Long Horizon

A Novel

by

S. A. Monkress

This is a work of fiction.

Some people mentioned in historical facts were actual persons who lived during the time period covered, but the characters and events of this story are figments of the author's imagination.

*Long Horizon © 2008 by S. A. Townley-Monkress
All rights reserved. No part of this book may be reproduced or transmitted in any form or by any means, without prior permission in writing from the publisher.*

WGA Registration #1152404

First publication 2009

ISBN 978-0-557-05274-5

*Back cover photo:
Oklahoma Sunset © 2009 S. A. Townley-Monkress*

Sincere thanks to:

Carolynn Richmond

for all your encouragement

and

William G. Roark

for your critique and suggestions

Dedicated with love to three resourceful women:

Paula VanDora McCarey Greenwood

Betty Jo Greenwood Townley Thomas

and

Mary Alice Wilson Townley Elder

*May the gift of our arts
restore
pieces of our lost hearts.*

| CHAPTER ONE |

1914

Slowly the sky brightened from dark to gold, as a narrow ribbon of sun put the night to bed. A slice of sunlight *streaked* through the edges of the loose, eastern-facing door on a weathered building, illuminating the cracks like hundreds of glinting mirrors. The warmth kissed her face.

She smiled, stretched and yawned like a satisfied barn cat. The sun, life-giving, felt sensuous. Sleepily gazing around, she spied horse stalls, fresh hay littered with bridles, boots and jackets strewn about the sweet-smelling barn. Blackie whinnied softly to her.

Jumping to her feet, she frantically snatched up her scattered belongings. She jerked up the cuffs of worn, faded britches to struggle into her boots, watching *him* slowly open one eye. Trying to focus on what she was doing, he lazily rubbed sleep from his eyes.

"Good morning, Miss Jessie," he yawned. "It *is* morning, right?"

"Right you are, Mr. Morgan, and I've got to get out of here! How could we just fall asleep last night!? I should have been home *hours* ago; I'll really catch it when I get home. Especially if Ben's up already."

"Aw, it's real early," he replied.

"Yes, but Ben's an early riser."

Daniel deliciously stretched his six-foot frame. "Yeah, well, that warden brother of yours is always in the way, doing things he shouldn't be."

"No, he's not always 'doing things he shouldn't be' - you just consider him an interference to you this morning. He's probably checking the bank statements and supplies, getting ready for today's work. You of all people should know there's nothing wrong with working hard."

He grinned. "Well, aren't we the defensive sister today!? Just last night you were griping about the reins being too tight."

She smiled impishly. "I guess that's just a woman's prerogative -- to do as she feels in one instance and different in the next. Besides, you know how it is with family -- you beat up on each other, but you don't let anyone else do it. Anyway, I really don't have time to debate with you right now; I've got to get out of here."

He took a moment to admire the way those britches fit those curves – figured they must be a pair of her younger brother's. He wouldn't like most women in men's pants, *but on her ... um ...!*

"Just as soon as you give me a kiss, you can go," he mocked.

Punishing her foot abruptly halted, as it finally slid down into the second boot. Running her fingers through her tussled hair, she unbolted the stall door and led Blackie out. "Sorry, Danny; that will have to wait." An instant later he heard the barn door slam after her.

Blast it! I'm supposed to be the one on the run, not this little flip of a woman. Most women would linger in his company, whine and pout, wanting more of his time. But not this little firecracker - she was always in a hurry. *And always leaving him wanting more.*

Daniel lazed back on the straw bed for a few minutes more, then struggled up and starting moving around. He knew if he dozed back off, he'd be dreaming again of silky, strawberry-hued hair and green eyes when he should be getting to work.

"Jessie McCarey, you drive me *CRAZY*," he said aloud.

-∞-

After Jessie gingerly urged her horse down the steep, rocky slope toward home, she crossed a grassy hillside sweeping downward into a charming valley blanketed with Lazy-Susans and other multi-colored wildflowers. The sun began its ascent into the sky. Overhead -- it was already no longer black, nor even deepest blue, but a clean azure.

Normally, she would delight in this early ride through the Oklahoma countryside. She'd suck in the fresh air, marvel at the sun painting those gorgeous golden/hot pink shades through the clouds, mimic catbirds with their meowing song and revel in the gold and green mixtures of wild scrub oak trees. Or indulge her dangerous spirit by galloping Blackie pell-mell around the sharp curve toward home. But right now: it felt as if the entire world were momentarily preserved in amber. Pushing Blackie, still she experienced a slow-motion sensation.

Jessie wondered whether Ben would be in a decent mood. Lately, he'd been an ogre and she suspected that financially their family may be hurting. She didn't want to cause him any more grief, but he had really been coming down on her. If he realized she hadn't been home … he'd be in a stormy mood this morning. Never before had she stayed out all night. Now she felt apprehensive as she quickly turned Blackie up the road leading to the picturesque house.

It always surprised her how much the view affected her, each time rounding that last bend. Spying their home from the long road momentarily brought her out of her stupor. Bright sunflowers and wild grasses sprang riotously all along the path and huge maple trees surrounding the house framed it like delicate filigree around a painting.

Papa really knew how to build us a home. She loved the way the full-circle porch wrapped around the warm-colored wood two-story. Her thoughts unexpectedly flooded with lively childhood memories of playing 'nurse' there with her headless doll (parts neglectfully lost); but preferring to chase after her brothers, wanting to join whatever *they* were engaged in.

Tying Blackie in the barn, she hastily entered the back door and tiptoed down the hallway to the room used as an office, listening for sounds that would indicate her oldest brother was awake. The long clock in the hall ticked … ticked … ticked, guiltily suggesting someone might be watching and waiting. Nearing the office, she heard the click of the old abacus. She took a deep breath and walked in.

Ben, so engrossed in a document he was studying on the desk, didn't notice her right off. She softly strolled next to him and laid her hand on his broad shoulder. He glanced up and smiled -- a good sign, so she playfully entwined her fingers into the blond curl at the back of his neck.

"How do things look?" Jessie asked.

"Not so good, kid."

Jessie was stunned; not surprised that the finances might be in poor shape, but that Ben never indicated anything negative about the family's business.

"What's wrong?"

He glanced up. For a minute, Jessie thought he would speak, but then, as if deciding how to say something, slowly shook his head.

Finally: "We're going to have to get into something else; this ranch just isn't making money. We're barely making ends meet and I can't keep Papa from spendin' money. Those Appaloosa ponies he bought last month just about did us in. I still haven't figured out *why* he bought them – they're not going to sell."

Jessie quit playing with his hair, surprised at Ben's revelation. "Can't believe you're telling me this; you never let me in on business."

"Well, *you* I can trust enough to tell and the only one with sense enough to understand these figures. The others, 'cept maybe Stephen, would only shrug it off with 'it'll all come out in the wash' or something else about as profound! Stephen is so busy working and trying to pay for school, I hate to worry him. I'm glad you're here, Jess – maybe you can help me figure out what to do with this mess."

Jessie stared at Ben with unabashed admiration, suddenly experiencing that bond she hadn't felt for awhile. She'd always looked up to her hulking oldest brother. And Ben was such an easy-going teddy bear; he and Jessie usually got along well. But lately he'd played the bossy brother card a lot. She might normally have thought it sweet – perhaps just protective of him, but lately it felt … confining.

"Aren't you going to ask me where I've been all night?"

"No, last night Mama said you were with Daniel Morgan. Why, I don't know, but my opinion of that arrogant … won't change anything, so I guess it doesn't matter. I thought you were still out when I got up and I worried, but hoped you had enough sense to get in here soon. If you hadn't come draggin' in before the folks ask about you, I'd have come looking for you. Wouldn't relish telling Mama her sweet daughter had been out *all* night."

"Yes, I was with Danny and for the obvious reasons - the same ones you and our dear brothers use when you're off with your women friends. I needed some company. I get the feeling you don't care much for him, but I feel safe with Danny. Because of his Daddy's reputation, if nothing else, you know he wouldn't let anything happen to me."

When Ben sighed, she softened her defensive stance: "I honestly meant to get in early, but we fell asleep. I'm sorry I worried you."

He narrowed his glance as he examined the expression on her face: very matter-of-fact, not all 'day-dreamy' as you'd expect from a young woman who might be carrying on an intimate relationship with a man. And Daniel Morgan wasn't the first, either; there was that wild Carston guy before. She acted just like a man, doing exactly as she pleased, and Ben felt she recklessly cared less what other people thought of her.

That bothered Ben a lot, but he knew better than to argue - it would only serve to make her more stubborn. Reasoning with her seemed a better solution. *But she's only seventeen!* He tried being responsible for her but she was a handful. Papa had her thoroughly spoiled. His only hope was that she'd get married and settle down, soon.

"Ben, please don't start lecturing me again. Tom is even worse and it's driving me crazy. I'd rather just help you today, with whatever needs to be done."

"Jess, you're just a kid and it frustrates me. If anything bad happened to you, I'd never forgive myself. As the oldest brother, I'm supposed to be your protector, do you know that? It puts me in a bad position – I want you to be happy and have fun, but where do I draw the line? Do you <u>know</u> what I'm sayin'?" He gave her a curious look.

"Yes, I understand perfectly what you mean. Ben, *nothing* happened between Danny and me."

When a disbelieving look appeared on his face: "*Really*! We'd been out riding along Ridge Road and stopped by that old barn of his cousin's. It was warm, so I pulled off my boots and relaxed, just looking up at the stars through the cracks. Good thing it didn't rain! Of course, then I'd probably not overslept …"

She giggled. "With my head on his shoulder … now, don't tell him, but instead of listening to his ramblings on and on about his father's bank, I kept going over in my mind all the legal work I'm learning. I was so tired; guess I just drifted off. Next thing I know, it's daybreak, so I hurtled home. Poor Blackie! I slipped in so you'd know I'm here, but need to go brush him down."

Jessie laid her hand on his shoulder again. "Honest: I *am* sorry."

She wished for some sort of understanding, or at least, resignation, of her right to a personal life. She knew, as a man, it would be difficult for her brother to empathize with her feelings, but still, she hoped ... *Papa* always seemed to trust her judgment ... Of course; she hadn't given him this particular reason not to trust her before.

He searched her pleading face for awhile, then reached up and clasped her hand in his. A smile lit up her face as she sighed - she had a reprieve for now; he wouldn't mention it to the folks.

"Ben, it's curious that you told me all this right now, because I've got an idea I'd like to talk to *you* about. Might even be a solution to our money problems. But first, I'll take care of Blackie."

"Mama will be cookin' breakfast soon; think I hear the others stirring." Ben reluctantly joined the conspiracy: "You best hurry; she'll wonder where you are. Meet ya in the kitchen -- I'm starving."

Ben slid his arm around her waist as they tiptoed down the long hallway, past family photos, wild flower arrangements and mementos. Ben gave Jessie an affectionate swat and shoved her out the side door as he headed toward the kitchen.

-∞-

A little later, Jessie returned via the kitchen door. There the windows were open, the morning breeze floating past bright yellow gingham curtains. Her brothers scattered around the large table, laughing and talking.

Tom, tall, muscular and with darker hair, was their next-to-the-oldest sibling. Reserved, and though very capable in many aspects, not exactly an introvert; but not a talker, either -- more of an action fellow, who prized the ranch life and working horses. He periodically ejected exasperated looks across the table at his younger siblings.

Next to Tom sat Stephen: articulate, dangerously handsome, thoughtful and intelligent. The studious member of the clan, Stephen eagerly anticipated attending law school. Stephen smiled at Tom's efforts to coral the on-going activity.

The twins, Jason and Josh, playfully wrestled; quite rambunctious at fifteen – typical rowdy boys. They looked very much alike, though not identical. Jason had startling-green eyes, whereas Josh's were blue-green. And one of Josh's front teeth protruded slightly in a different direction, sporting a chip from an earlier tussle with his twin. But their similar mannerisms, frequent grins, freckles and light-brown hair stuck up in the same cowlick in back, often giving folks pause, trying to determine which ornery youngster they were dealing with.

And of course, the youngest: eleven-year-old Matthew, (though he would be furious if called the 'baby.') Matt didn't sit down at the table; instead, he followed his mother around the kitchen like a sweet little puppy, begging to help.

Their mother, Kathleen, a stunning, forty-ish auburn-haired woman, busily fried eggs and sizzling slab bacon in huge cast-iron skillets over the wood-heated stove. She reached up and brushed a pretty tendril from her face, where it escaped from the mother-of-pearl clasp holding her hair back from the nape of her delicate neck. As she pulled open an oven door to take out hot biscuits, the delicious smell filled the room.

"U-m!" Jessie enthused and their Mama glanced up from her work.

Ben stood lackadaisically in the doorway, and Jessie smiled up at him and snuggled against his shoulder - a rare sight lately. The twins stopped their playful wrestling momentarily when they spied Jessie and Ben.

"Just what're ya'll up to?" Jason asked.

"Oh, we're ... being conspiratorial," she answered.

"Con, conspir... what? Why don't ya just speak English, Jessie? Always showing off that teacher instinct!"

"I'm not going to be a teacher, and you know it! I don't have enough patience with children. Why do you keep bugging me about that?"

"Well, you wus offered that job teaching grammar school; had the best grades for several years and finished way ahead of us. Ya always made better grades 'an us."

"*You'd* do better if you brought work home in each subject every night like I did …"

Jason playfully popped his napkin at her. "I'm s'prised ya don't take 'vantage of that job offer."

"I'll take advantage of something!" She reached over and rubbed his hair around and around, reducing the fair stuff to a static-icky mess.

"Hey!" he started, but she grabbed him from behind, putting her arm around his neck in a mock headlock.

"Don't mess with me, boy, or I'll have to make you look bad!"

The commotion was suddenly interrupted with: "*Sarah Jessica McCarey*! Why must you continue to roughhouse with your brothers? It's so unladylike! It was bad enough when you were little, but you're a grown woman!"

Kathleen McCarey never employed the masculine-sounding shortening of her daughter's middle name that her husband and sons used. *It just wasn't fitting.* And when Kathleen became perturbed with any of her children ... the complete name was ejected. The intended offspring immediately recognized the need to snap to attention.

Jason looked up at Jessie and grimaced - he knew he was partly responsible for her getting the reprimand. *Sorry*, his eyes seemed to say.

"Yes, Mama," Jessie sighed, "but it's so much fun to tease him."

Her mother sighed in return. *Would she ever understand this wild daughter?*

Kathleen McCarey was a beautiful woman - still. Small, a couple of inches shorter than her daughter and slender, even at forty-seven, after having borne seven children. She had very fair, smooth skin with just a hint of freckles across her nose, and still-brilliant dark, copper-colored hair. Kathleen was the true southern woman: feminine, soft-spoken, family-oriented and very conservative; fragile-looking, yet strong. Her husband and children adored her and she centered her entire life -- every waking moment -- on their needs.

Jessie's Mother pretty much understood her sons, they were, after all ... *men. But Sarah!* How she longed for her only daughter to share companionly, womanly things with her - cooking, sewing, talking together about the things in their hearts. But her daughter much preferred to be out with her father and the boys - working the horses or anything other than being in the house. *Not that Sarah wasn't a dutiful daughter.* She did her share of the work. Sarah didn't have to be asked to help with pumping and carrying water from the cistern, or the washing and ironing, mending or cleaning. She was always the first to jump in when she saw something that needed to be done. But she didn't take the pride in keeping house that Kathleen did.

To Kathleen, keeping the house was akin to spirituality; she cooked, made beds, cleaned, organized, and repaired the children's clothes painstakingly and lovingly. But not her daughter - she finished the work as quickly as she could so she could be off outside with the men. Though she had a healthy appetite, obviously Sarah didn't enjoy the cooking.

And that job of Sarah's! No self-respecting woman had to work to support herself - even though it was for a highly-regarded man like Wayne McPherson, the local lawyer. Kathleen was proud of her daughter's book learning, but secretly worried that Sarah would never be able to catch a good man. Little did she know that the farthest thing from Jessie's mind was getting a man to 'take care of her.'

"I thought you'd be downstairs to help me earlier. Have you been out riding?"

"Y…es, Mama. I…'m sorry; didn't realize the time. I'll set the table," Jessie guiltily volunteered.

As she pulled plates and cups from the bureau, Jessie cradled one of the plates – lovingly caressing it with her fingers. She stroked the light gold filigree on its edges, then across the scene of a stunningly beautiful lady in fancy ballroom dress. This was one of two surviving china plates belonging to her great grandmother, Bridgette, when she was a young bride in Ireland. Jessie had always admired the delicate items and cherished them as treasured possessions.

She wistfully envisioned their Grandmother carefully placing them around the table for her own family. "How I'd love to travel to Ireland, and find out about our great grandparents."

"When you go, can I come along?" Matthew wheedled.

Jessie smiled. "Sure, Buddy."

Jessie decided to place the two plates at the back of the stack of dishes in the cupboard, so they wouldn't receive as much wear.

"Mama, we should find a way to display Grandmere's plates, to keep them looking nice. If we keep washing them so much, the exquisite prints will disappear. They're antiques -- to me, anyway."

Kathleen's face brightened. "That's a lovely idea, sweetheart. Perhaps we could crochet a hangar for the wall?"

Matthew, with a wide grin, eagerly reached across the table. Mimicking Jessie's gestures, he helped place everything on the table just as Jessie did. "Thanks, Matty," she beamed at the younger brother she adored.

Matthew had sandy-colored curls, big blue eyes and the sweetest smile she ever beheld. Ever since he was born, Jessie could never get enough of hugging and holding him. His long lashes would brush her cheek while rocking him – she thought of them as angel kisses.

Actually, all the McCarey siblings spoiled him – gave him their rare treats of candy, rides on their shoulders, nearly anything he wanted. But rather than acting badly, Matt had such a sweet disposition, few could resist his smile. Jessie hoped he'd always be this way and nothing would ever hurt him or change his innocent exuberance for those people and things he loved. As Matt rounded the corner of the table, the twins grabbed him, tickling him mercilessly as they pulled him up to sit between them.

Jessie made several trips to the table, carrying dishes, homemade blackberry jam, biscuits. She grabbed the coffee pot and filled everyone's cups, (Matt's small one only half-way, the other half -- milk), just as Gus McCarey walked into the kitchen. Gus was such a big man; he seemed to fill the colossal oak frame of the doorway.

"Coffee, Papa?"

"Yes, my Darlin'; and how is everyone this lovely mornin'?"

All eyes gravitated to the graying-blond man standing at the head of the table. He'd had another bout of drinking last night, so they were somewhat surprised at his lilting mood.

"We're all good, Papa," Jason answered. "What do you think we should start first today? Plenty to do. Josh and I were just figurin' who would be fixin' those fences on the south end today and who all would be gelding..."

Gus looked blankly at him.

"You remember; we talked about the colts yesterday, Papa."

"Oh? ... Oh! Yes, I forget, you're exactly right, son."

The room got very quiet as they assessed this most-recent of their father's lapses. They seemed to be getting more and more frequent. And their father seemed to be doing less and less around the ranch. It wasn't as though he was lazy – it was ... something they couldn't put their finger on – more like disinterest or inattentiveness. They all felt Papa simply too young to be getting senile, so it was puzzling and a little worrisome.

The silence was finally broken by Kathleen's sweet voice: "And how much do you think you can eat this morning, dear?"

"Plenty!" Then, rubbing his hands in anticipation, he sat down.

After grace, the chatter soon began again around the table; a little jabbing of each other, affectionate horseplay with the passing of food, until Kathleen would give them an exasperated look. Which would halt it temporarily -- typical mealtime at the McCareys.

-∞-

As soon as everyone finished breakfast, Jessie excused herself and led Ben back to the study.

"OK," she said, taking a deep breath, "before you show me our desperate condition on the ranch books, you ready for this?"

"I guess I might as well be - what's got you interested?"

"Oil"

"*Oil?*"

"Yes, oil."

"What *are* you talking about, Jessie?"

"I want us to get into the oil business."

She hesitated dramatically. Then: "You know, put up a rig and plunk a hole – *[she dropped her finger down from mid-air in an exaggerated gesture]* -- then oil pops out of the ground and we make money."

"Are you *crazy*? We don't know anything about drilling for oil!"

"What's there to know? None of the other drillers around here know what they're doing, either. Why do you think they call it 'wildcatting?' And I've been doing some research…"

"When would you have time to do that - what with your job at McPherson's office and helping Mama here, too?"

"On my lunch hours. I've been quizzing that guy who works for the Franks on their leases. He explained some interesting stuff about rocks and the lay of the land around here; called it the study of 'geology'. There are good areas for drilling oil here - probably some better than others. I've been listening to him and studying how the layers of rock form in certain spots. Think I know a good place to try."

"You lost me." Ben rubbed his forehead as if it hurt.

Scrambling around, she found a piece of paper and pencil in the desk and drew a sketch of layers of rock formations, like she'd seen the driller in town use. She showed Ben how the oil became trapped in spaces, and pockets or domes above, filled with gas. She explained that much of the recent theory about finding oil had been derived from earlier drilling for water in Pennsylvania.

"How'd you learn all this?" He may not have understood all of it, but Ben was apparently impressed with the drawing.

"Just listening - to him and others out there around the Franks' well. I go out quite a lot in the evening. They assume I'm just riding around, enjoying the fresh air - some dumb woman, but even when I'm not asking questions, I've been listening and taking notes on the sly. Had to be a bit secretive -- didn't want him to suspect that I was picking his brain."
She laughed.

"And just how to you propose to do this?"

"Well, we purchase a lease, get up a crew (mostly me, you, the other boys), build a rig and start drilling - just like the other wildcatters. I think we should talk to Samm Mann about leasing his property, to start. There's an area over there that looks like it may have one of those salt domes on it … see how the wide creek turns and swells here at the Indian trading post … all the silt built up. I think it would be worth checking out."

"You know Samm's turned down every prospective driller?"

"Yes, but I think he'll talk to us. I'll ride over soon and visit. [A *mischievous grin spread across her face.]* Maybe take some of Mama's fresh pumpkin bread as a bribe. We might try getting a 'stay' lease on the Smiths' property adjoining Samm's, in case a well comes in. You know how other drillers set up a rig as close to a find as possible, which depletes the pressure."

"Is that important …?"

"We'll want the option. If we hit oil, within days any open area surrounding Samm will disappear under a maze of derricks and the tents of the wheeler-dealers, conmen and others looking to find an easy buck."

"Sounds mighty ambitious. All this takes money - where you

gonna get it?"

"I've got most of mine saved up from the last three summers working. Thought you might have a little, too? We need enough to travel to Kansas City or St. Louis - to try to get some investors to help put up the needed capital."

When Ben looked puzzled she added: "You know, buyer friends of Papa's."

"Capital?"

"Money!"

"You think you can just waltz up there and people are gonna give you money to punch holes in the ground?!!"

"Yes, they will. Of course, we have to convince them there's money to be made here - and *right now* before it's all drilled out. I've got some good ideas and selling points."

"They'd never listen to a woman."

"I figured that." She sighed. "I'll coach Stephen until he can discuss this like I would. Even better. You know he's got the gift of gab. Then we'll send you and him to negotiate with them."

"Jess, I don't know ..."

"Yes, you do - we've got to grab this opportunity, Ben, right now! Ben, be bold - *we can do this*! *Please* do this with me!"

Her radiant face pleaded with him. He'd not seen her like this since the day she first learned to gallop Blackie pell-mell across the range, hair flying - eyes dancing. He shook his head, exasperated.

"Stay with me, now, Ben; listen to me. I've got a lot more ideas about this. We can do this!"

"Well, let's get Stephen in here and see what he thinks, if he hasn't already left for town." Ben nodded toward the door.

"I think I just heard him talking to the twins. He probably does need to leave, so why don't I tell him we'd like to talk to him when he gets off work?" Jessie asked.

"Okay, that will give you and me awhile to hash over some more of your 'ideas'. Although I still don't know, Jessie …"

"You will by the time I'm finished with you!! I'm not going to give up, particularly now that I can see I have you interested. And I think Messrs. Martin and Stockton will be intrigued when we talk with them," she countered.

Jessie walked outside on the wide porch and found Stephen saddled up as expected, ready to leave for town.

"Brilliant Brother, Ben and I need to discuss some business with you this evenin' after work, so come right on home, o'kay?"

"What about, Jessie?"

"Oh, you'll find out … [*she smiled mischievously*]… tonight."

"Got to tease me, huh, Orn'ry?" Stephen laughed.

He turned and lifted himself onto his horse, then trotted out toward Big Spring, the town two miles away. She watched his tall frame disappear down the road; thinking to herself: *yes, Stephen would be the right man to influence the investors*. Naturally, as head of the family and this prospective venture, Ben would go also, but Stephen was the man for this job – he worked very hard at school and struggled with two part-time jobs to save for tuition so he could go back to university. She was so proud of him for continuing his education.

And Stephen had a personable way about him. People liked him right off; felt comfortable with him. *Gosh, he might be a politician or judge or even governor someday*! But for now her only concern: that Stephen convinces a few choice people -- backers -- to part with some of their hard-earned dollars. She felt confident that they wouldn't be wasting their money. *It's gonna get interesting ...!*

Now, she needed to convince Stephen and make sure that Ben understood why Stephen should do the major part of the presentation. She loved them both so much; she couldn't bear the thought of ever hurting either of them.

-∞-

When Stephen returned home that evening, Jessie had Ben convinced that they should at least *try* to see whether her proposed business venture would work. After supper, they all strolled outside and Jessie hopped up on the corral fence, relishing the gorgeous April evening and brimming with excitement, especially now that Ben was an ally. The men pulled out cigars and began puffing -- Stephen offering Jessie one in jest.

"No, thanks," she sweetly declined.

"Why not - you try everything else we do," he joked.

"Well, to tell you the truth, I smoked tobacco once, but it didn't appeal to me. Made me cough and it *stinks.* If you've got some whiskey, though, I'll try that." She grimaced, and then smiled sweetly.

While Stephen roared with laughter, Ben just shook his head. This wild sister of theirs! *Now what is she getting them into?*

Jessie started: "Stephen, Ben and I have been discussing a little money-making project we'd like you involved in."

"Yeah, what do you have in mind, Sis?"

"You know that gusher the Townsends brought in last week? I think we should find some money and start doing some drilling for oil ourselves. This area must be rich with it." Stomping her boots on the ground: "I just *sense* there's a whole lot more in there."

"Whoa, that's quite an idea, Jessie. I don't know ..."

"Before you start getting pessimistic, let me tell you what I think we can do."

"What do you think of this idea, Ben?" Stephen quizzed. "Yours or hers?"

"I have to give her full credit," Ben admitted. "At first, I was really skeptical, too, but she's convinced me that we ought to go for it. Give her a chance to explain, okay?"

"Lay it on me, Sis."

Jessie proceeded to show Stephen about the geology and how to interest investors, as she'd explained to Ben earlier. When she finished, Stephen had a few questions but seemed incredibly optimistic. Jessie breathed a sigh of relief - *he hadn't been as hard to sell as Ben.*

"I don't have any cash I can put in, Jessie. You know I have tuition to pay, but if you and Ben can come up with the travel money, I'll be happy to go to St. Louis or Kansas City and try convincing those investors. May be able to get my boss to let me be away for a few days; but not long, for sure. While I talk to him, you two get the rest of the plans worked up."

Suddenly, Stephen grinned broadly. "You know, I'm getting kinda excited about this!"

Jessie thrilled to hear him say that - she felt confident now that Stephen would come home with the money they needed.

She turned to their oldest brother. "Ben, you understand ... don't you ... why I think Stephen should do the presentation? I know you're head of the family and all ..."

"Stephen will do a great job, Jess – and he's welcome to the job. Anyhow, I get nervous talking in front of a group; but he's a natural. I'll back him up with the figures; that's what *I'm* good at."

She reached over and hugged him. "By the way, we'll get the other boys involved later if they want, but for right now, this is just between the three of us? The others will assume you're selling some horses. If things don't work out, all we'll be out is our own savings. I really hate to hold out on Tom, but I'm afraid he might be too negative and we don't need that. When we get the cash and are ready to do the actual work, we'll ask for his advice. But for now, let's keep mum, okay?"

When Jessie winked, the three nodded in agreement, grinning at each other like ornery little kids who had entered into a secret pact.

| CHAPTER TWO |

Two weeks later, Jessie drove Ben and Stephen in the wagon down the rutted road toward the train station in Big Spring. The men bantered light-heartedly back and forth to each other; Jessie apprehensive -- deep in thought. Over and over in her mind, she scrutinized the proposal.

For a little relief when they reached the busy station, she watched people saying their goodbyes. Jessie loved studying people. The differences were fascinating: some excited; others -- teary-eyed. She experienced sadness at one mother's poignant goodbye to a son leaving for his army obligations. Others she didn't know, so she concocted their stories in her mind. She often fantasized about what adventures they were off to. How she longed to escape with some of them, and see what existed outside this territory. Of course, if her plan came to fruition, she should have some exciting adventures right here!

She finally chided herself: *This is it. We've done everything we can.* All the preparatory work - written up a proposal showing where they thought good sites were located, estimated the initial drilling and start-up costs and discussed a contract with a driller she felt confident in -- recommended by a friend of theirs from school. She felt the figures were extremely realistic, so had faith that Stephen could sell their deal.

As her brothers took their luggage from the wagon, she began to interject a few last reminders, but Stephen cut her short: "I know, I know, get the 'hook' in them about Oklahoma being 'the land of opportunity' before we show the figures; make the point of the realistic expense versus profit ratio; don't let them negotiate too high a percentage for their investment; blah, blah, blah! I've got this *down*, Jess. Don't worry, Honey."

"Stephen's right, Jessie, he's going to do real fine and I can finagle the figures. It'll work out," Ben soothed.

"I know, I'm sorry, I'm just so excited. I wish ..." she looked wistfully at them, "... I could go, too, but ... oh well; I've got work to do here, anyway."

Stephen looked for a moment at her upturned face. "Next time, we'll take you, Jess. Promise."

She smiled, hugged them both and waved them off on their adventure. Lingering until the train was no longer in sight, she knew she'd indulged in enough self-pity, so she headed home. Like she told her brothers, she had work to do. So she best get busy.

-∞-

The next day, as soon as she finished chores around the house for Mama, Jessie rode Blackie out around the winding curve of the Sandy River bend to see Samm Mann. This time, rather than seemingly oblivious to the raw Oklahoma natural beauty, she reveled in it, trying to prepare what she would say. Jessie innately breathed the special mystique of this part of the country. She couldn't imagine living anywhere else. A spiritual love for this rich, red land – was something she shared with Samm.

Sitting outside his small, lean-to house, sorting seed corn, Samm wasn't expecting her, but he never seemed surprised any time she rode up. To an observer, it would appear that he disliked her; he said absolutely nothing all the while she tied up her horse and approached. But that was just his way; Jessie understood.

"Hello, Samm." Jessie smiled, and waited patiently.

After a while: "Little bird ... have you again flown away from the nest?" Samm tried to hide a smile. A reclusive man, perhaps because he was half Cherokee, he wasn't the type to deal with most 'outsiders'. But he had known the McCarey family a long time and respected Gus McCarey.

Though he'd never admit it, Samm was fond of Jessie. She'd ridden over to his place by herself, ever since she was small. Samm hadn't known what to think of her at first, always tagging after him like a little lost puppy, but her persistence paid off: finally, he warmed to her. She had been fascinated with his family history, respectfully asking him countless questions about them, all the while quietly helping with whatever he was doing without being in the way. So he came to think her 'acceptable.'

"I have a present for you." She handed him a wrapped bundle.

He breathed in deeply of the gift and smiled. He prized Mrs. McCarey's fresh bread.

"And also a favor to ask."

When Samm looked inquisitively at Jessie, she sucked in her

breath. To many, he may have been 'just an Injun', but she recognized Samm as a man of penetrating intelligence. She knew she should just jump in -- *Don't hem and haw around the bush; Samm can see right through people.*

"Actually, the request is like ... a business proposal."

"Don't have more horses broken yet, little one ..."

"That's not why I've come, Samm. It's other business. And ... right off: I want you to know I've thought hard and carefully about it. Wish it was something we could do on our property and not have to bother you, but I believe your land is more promising."

Jessie hesitated awhile, but as expected, Samm wouldn't ask anything. He went back to sorting the corn. Most times, talking to him was like pulling teeth. She must initiate and lead the conversation -- she was on her own here. Taking a deep breath, she jumped in rapidly:

"Samm, I know you aren't crazy about the idea of drilling for oil around here. But I've studied this area and I'm convinced your property has a good pool beneath it. Ben and Stephen are trying to get investors to partner with us, and we want you to be our partner, too."

"Little Bird, oil is dirty. Stupid white men tear up the land and leave it dirty."

"Yes, some do. But you know our family and how we keep our property. We would respect your land and once the drilling is complete – we'd pull the rig out, clean up all the mess, even attempt to plant something around the site. The area I'm interested in isn't near your crops or your water supply – it's over close to that bare ravine where nothing grows but scrub brush."

"That filthy black stuff runs all over. After it's outta the hole, can't clean it up. Ruins the land."

Jessie looked up at Samm with the pleading little pout she frequently utilized.

"If I say we will clean it up, won't you believe me? We'll research it and find the best way. You know we're good as our word."

"I know your family is truthful. But you can't stop the mess. I seen that filthy oil rise way into the sky for a long time. It's too much dirty."

Jessie responded: "But that's if it isn't contained. I promise … before we ever would begin to drill, we'll investigate how to stop it and contain it, as soon as we can when it gushes. Perhaps Tom can experiment with some type of fittings. After all, why would we want to waste it? We've heard of that happening, Samm. I don't want to ruin your property, or waste the oil. I can't promise it won't run onto the ground at first, but … if we do everything we can to minimize the spill, will you at least consider this?"

To Jessie, it seemed an eternity passed.

"I will need time to think."

"Thank you, my friend; I completely understand. When Ben returns from his trip north, I'll have him come over and talk to you more. And you know we'd give you a fair price. We don't want to take advantage of you, or anyone else for that matter. If we're going to start this business, I want to do it right."

Jessie again reassured him that they would clean his land, once they had finished with the drilling.

"Little Bird, why is this so important to you? You have a nice home, nice land, nice family. Someday you will marry and run busy, caring for your own hard-headed little ones."

Jessie laughed. "Don't marry me off right away, Samm. For awhile, I'd like to see what it's like to have opportunities like a man. I know that probably sounds like crazy talk, but I have this … Uh, this …"

"Fire?"

"Yes! That's it -- a fire inside me. I can't explain it. Not to my brothers; and especially not to Mama. Perhaps Papa senses what I need. He lets me try lots of things most fathers wouldn't put up with in their daughters."

"It's your spirit – wild, like fire in the wind."

When Samm chuckled uncharacteristically, Jessie knew he'd eventually come around.

"And just think … you could build that extra room Asinka's been wanting with the money!"

-∞-

A few days later, Jessie spoke with Samm again. He finally agreed and they negotiated a fee for leasing his property that she believed reasonable from both parties' viewpoint. If they were going to succeed, she was adamant that they shouldn't take advantage of others.

-∞-

By the time for Ben and Stephen's return, Jessie was nearly beside herself, wondering how they had fared with the northern businessmen. She felt Chauncey Martin would be fairly easy to convince; he was a modern man and always looking for promising new business. But David Stockton was tough; he'd earned his money the hard way -- starting as a stable boy, learning the horse trade until he made enough money to start his own ranch. Jessie admired Mr. Stockton's conservative business acumen.

Jessie had also bantered with the driller again. Not because he was anxious to work with her, but because he didn't presently have any work lined up, he reluctantly said he'd *likely* be available. But wanted to talk to Ben.

A lot of recent drilling had occurred north and west of Big Spring, over in '*the Osage*'. Osage County enclosed one of the richest areas for productive leases. However, due to Federal law, those had to be negotiated with the Indian tribe and from what she had gleaned from other drillers, could be quite expensive.

Auctions were held outside the Tribal office in Pawhuska, under what was called 'the million dollar elm' because of the high demand for purchasing drilling rights on Osage leases. If her family successfully discovered a good site, perhaps later they could afford to bid for a lease there. That idea fascinated Jessie. However, drilling right here in Spring County, they could negotiate directly through the landowner. And Samm had finally relented! Now if her brothers' trip was successful …

-∞-

As she waited [way too early] at the train depot to pick up her brothers, Jessie's mind raced, anxious. To bide the time, she grabbed the folded paper from her back pocket and began jotting down notes: *-hire work hands, -talk to Tom about building the rig, - slow the oil??- how to contain it? -set up record books, -look over the proposed site again, -get Samm to come out to the area to see exactly what we do.*

Finally, against a cirrus cloud, dazzling blue sky, the tell-tale billows of spewing steam from the train came into sight. It seemed to roll on forever, shouting its loud arrival, but eventually stopped. She examined the sea of faces departing. Soon, she recognized Ben's tall frame jump from the doorway exit, with Stephen following. They glanced up and down the tracks and located her, also. They waved. She anxiously watched their faces all the while they approached, to see whether they were in a positive mood.

Oh no! They're not smiling; they're not excited! She watched Stephen jerk loose the black ribbon tie at his collar, but couldn't detect any type of emotion.

When they reached her, Stephen embraced her, then proceeded to throw his beat-up old suitcase over into the wagon. Ben did the same. Not a word; it was driving her mad!

"OK, you two. Tell me. Tell me *right now*!!"

Stephen glanced at Ben, who shrugged his shoulders as if to say, *go ahead and tell her*. Then Stephen's face broke into a huge grin as he pulled cheques and contracts from his coat pocket. "Signed, sealed and delivered,

Sis; we did it!"

Jessie screamed like a banshee and threw her arms around his neck in a fierce hug. Stephen swung her around, letting let her down beside Ben. She embraced Ben, and then hooked her arms into each of theirs. "This calls for a celebration! What ya say? Let's go into town for a cold drink -- my treat!"

Stephen responded, "I'm on."

Ben retorted, "Only place to get something cold is the tavern – but it's rough, especially lately, with all the riff-raff swarming into Big Spring. I don't think we should take her in there."

Jessie pleaded: "This is a special occasion for all of us. I persuaded Samm, too, though he seemed quite leery at first. I've got lots to tell you before we go home! Please, Ben!"

Ben stalled. "Drinking in the middle of the day?"

Jessie wrangled: "Would probably be quiet now; most folks are busy at work. Oh, come on, Ben. It'll be all right. I've got two big brothers to take care of me. It'll be a real adventure, please, *please* take me!"

Ben looked at her pleading face; understanding exactly why Papa had such a hard time telling her *NO*. Jessie was hard to refuse when she was acquiescent like this – a rare sight. Stephen laughed, so Ben finally relented and she rewarded him by her snuggling his arm as they strolled down the dust-hazed bare street toward the tavern.

Jessie took great pleasure in coming to town; the initial reason (besides the spending money) she began working for Mr. McPherson. She loved the ranch and being outdoors with her father and brothers, but also relished the companionable buzz of conversation and contact with the townspeople.

They passed *Jeremiah's General Store*, which now also housed the post office. A bustling, large, two-story building with a wooden porch built all the way around; they spied the busy storekeeper sweeping whittling scraps off the porch.

"Hey Jeremiah, you ought-a stock some bottles of cold soda pop in your store," Stephen suggested.

"Think so?"

"Sure, when it's warm outside like today, would sell like hotcakes. You could get ice from Andy's icehouse over on Second Street."

"Might be perty expensive. But maybe I'll think on it."

People smiled and chatted to them as they passed – Mrs. Lowry and the three rowdy children she was failing to control; Melvin, the butcher from the end of the block; elderly men spitting and whittling on wooden porches. Carl, the town's lone constable, tipped his hat to them, smiling all the while appreciatively eying Jessie.

"Carl," Jessie cantankerously called to him, "You been catchin' any desperate outlaws lately?"

Carl picked up on her teasing and blushed unexpectedly. "Miss Jessie, ya best behave yo'self – or I might have to lock ya up in that there jailhouse." He jerked his head in a quick motion toward a barred window across the street.

She laughed: "I'll try real hard to be good."

"Yeah ... right."

The three siblings continued strolling down the street; Jessie visibly excited. *Things are really coming together in Big Spring*! She felt like pinching herself to make sure she was awake. Jessie watched as people passed by - shopkeepers, drillers, roughnecks, all sorts of new folks. She was fascinated by the eclectic scene before her: here, a child's wagon loaded with tools. Beside that, a plot growing tomatoes anchored to wooden stakes with ragged pieces of cloth. Only a few feet down sprawled the new bank, a stunningly-beautiful example of large, limestone architecture contrasted with glistening glass windows. Across the road, horses were tied to hitching posts, right alongside a few horseless buggies 'parked' awkwardly at various angles.

What a boiling pot of diverse people! Jessie kept thinking: *Such an exciting time to be alive - so much happening and the town growing so quickly! Just think how great this street would look if it were bricked!* She knew instinctively that more and more businesses and buildings would spring up all along its sides.

Oblivious to the attention she created when she walked inside the dimly-lit tavern with her brothers; Jessie was too intrigued taking it all in. The bar, made of crude wooden crates, had a thickly-varnished wooden slab across the top which the bartender used to slide drinks down to the customers. A huge mirror edged in gold colored trim reflected the seated customers. To the right a shelf stocked various bottles of liquor. The windows were covered with dark red velvet curtains. Jessie supposed that an attempt to make the place look elegant, but laughed to herself at the barkeep's effort. It was all pretty crude and gaudy, but she was enjoying herself nonetheless.

Most of the occupants were dusty and grimy, probably roustabout employees of the wildcatters. Some were local ranchers and farmers. Not used to seeing many women coming into the tavern, mostly just the rough-looking girls who worked tables, a couple of the men stared unabashedly at Jessie in her girlish pale yellow blouse and riding skirt. Several appreciative gestures and murmurs occurred. Ben noticed right off and became nervously protective.

"Where do you want to sit? How about over there in the corner?"

Jessie shook her head. "Oh, no, it's dark over there and we can't see anyone; let's sit here at the bar on these stools."

She quickly hopped up, indicated 'three' to the guy behind the bar and excitedly looked around, taking it all in like a kid in a candy store. Before Ben could counter for a Sarsaparilla for her, someone came up behind him and roughly tapped him on the shoulder.

Glancing around, Ben faced their brother Tom, sporting an extremely irritated look in his eyes. Next to Tom stood Daniel Morgan. Tom and Daniel had been sitting, unnoticed, at the back of the room and spied Ben, Jessie and Stephen when they walked in.

"What are you two doin,' bringin' Jessie in here? Have you lost your minds?!" Tom demanded.

"She wanted to come; we're sort of celebrating a little project the three of us are working on, so Stephen and I decided it was okay for a little while," Ben retorted defensively.

"What sort of celebration justifies you bringing her into a sleazy dump like this?"

Ben hesitated, looking over at Jessie, as if to say: *when are we going to tell him?*

Jessie stepped off the bar stool and stood directly in front of Tom. "Don't jump on Ben for bringing me in here! It's just a lark. But … I'll come in here by myself if I want to!" she exhorted loudly.

"Well, don't get your little temper in an uproar," backing off somewhat. "It's not very lady-like, that's all."

Daniel stood there, silently assessing the situation. His expression suggested his disapproval; obviously he, too, wasn't amused by Jessie's presence in the tavern.

"Well, I could care less of your opinion of my degree of 'lady-likeness'. Besides, there's no reason for fighting; we've got a plan to discuss with you, if you'll settle down and just behave yourself."

"A plan? What kinda plan?"

"How to make some money -- interested? No, wait a minute; before you say anything, you have to promise not to be pessimistic or have your usual 'down-in-the mouth' attitude, okay?"

Daniel addressed Jessie in a condescending tone: "I've really got to run right now, and it looks like you probably have some family situation to discuss. But I'll be talking to *you* later, Jessie."

"Okay," she absently responded, still preoccupied in her defiant stance at Tom. Daniel started to leave, but turned and hesitated, glancing back. Jessie barely acknowledged her friend's departure, which appeared to irritate Daniel even more. Finally, he sighed and strode out of the door.

She turned to Tom: "Come sit down with us and we'll tell you about our little venture."

Jessie motioned him to the bar but he firmly grabbed her arm, guiding her toward the back of the room, to the out-of-the-way table he'd shared with Daniel Morgan. Ben and Stephen picked up their cold drinks and followed.

"Okay, what're you up to?"

Jessie had begun to look around again in fascination. Tom snapped his fingers in front of her face to get her attention.

"Oh! Well, the boys and I have come up with some investment money and we're going to hire a driller and … start drilling for oil over on Samm Mann's property. Now, whatta ya think of that?"

Tom scratched his head, dazed for a minute before answering, "You've got money already? And how you gonna get Mann to let you drill?"

Jessie explained to him about their brothers' trip to St. Louis and Kansas City, about her plan for drilling, and her conversations with Samm Mann. Tom listened silently during the explanation, then asked, "Why haven't you told me before now?"

Before Jessie could answer, Stephen broke in: "Because you would just shoot us outta the sky, like you do everything else! We wanted to have a positive plan working before we involved you and Jason. Not that Jason would be as pessimistic as you; he's just been so busy helping Papa with the ranch. We thought we'd tell him when we were sure we could do this."

"Well, someone's got to be realistic around here," Tom defended.

Ben cut in: "Whoa, wait a minute there, 'little' brother. No one's more realistic than I am. Who do you think has worried about Papa's mis-management of the ranch for the last four years? I've had nothing but headaches, trying to pay the bills and keep us afloat. More than happy to show you the past year's records, if you'd spare me the time."

"No, sorry; I'll take your word for it. Didn't know things were that bad, but s'pected it wusn't great. So, ya think ya can make a go of this oil drilling thing, huh?"

Jessie enthused: "Yes, we can. It's a big risk, of course, but what isn't? And Tom, you're so good working around machinery and all, we'll *really* need your advice with the operations."

Ben interjected: "*Sure* we can make a go of this. Course, we'll all still have to work at the ranch, but we want to get the family involved as much as we can; won't have to hire so many hands. Let's get on home and get the twins inspired. Jason should be game; not sure about Josh. He keeps talking bout joinin' the blasted army when he's old enough. And Matt's a bit too young to be much help to us right now. Maybe Papa can use him to help feed horses at the ranch anyway. Worst thing is telling Papa; don't know how he'll take it."

They all silently nodded their heads in agreement. Jessie looked at each of them for some time, then started laughing. Soon they all joined in, amused that they actually agreed on something.

| CHAPTER THREE |

A couple of days later, the McCarey family relaxed and talked after supper. Jessie and Ben had piqued both the twins' interests in the drilling project. Jason and Josh were big for fifteen years old, so they would be handy. Since Matt was only eleven, he would be more useful staying at the ranch and helping their father for now. Josh offered to work a few hours a day at the lease, then head on home to see what their father needed done.

Jessie told the boys that she would help Ben oversee the activity and keep the business records, run errands and the like, and still try to do some of the housework with their mother. She intended to tell Mr. McPherson that she'd only be available for research in his office a few hours a week, if at all. She so enjoyed learning about the law, it saddened her that she'd need to have that conversation – more than likely her boss would need to hire someone else for her job.

Josh posed the inevitable question: "Since we'll be getting started building that rig next week, don't you think we should tell Papa what's going on?"

"*How* are we gonna tell him?" Jason asked skeptically.

Tom and Ben both spoke at the same time: "Yeah, Jessie? How

you gonna tell him?"

"*Me!!?* "Why *me*?"

"Well, it'll likely come easier from you - you know how he dotes on you," Tom opined.

Jessie stared at each of them, exasperated. Finally: "Oh -- all right. I've been sort of planning this out in my mind, anyway. How about this: I'll get Papa laughing and talking about the old days and once he's relaxed, we'll *ease* it in. You all be close by to lend moral support, and jump in when you see me floundering, okay?"

"O.K." was all they could muster.

"Let's head on into the sitting area. Papa's just staring out the window. Don't make a big production of us going in together. Let's just take turns slowly sauntering in and sitting down."

When Jessie and Ben strolled in first, she went over to her father and sat down next to him on the worn arm of his upholstered chair. He looked up at her and smiled. "Jessie, me Darlin', give your old Papa a kiss." Jessie tenderly kissed the weathered cheek and laid her head next to his, putting her arm comfortably around his shoulder.

When she noticed the others had settled in, she attempted a casual pose. "Papa, tell us again about the land rush of '93."

"I would think you'd be a'tired o'hearin' that old story."

"Oh, no, Papa, we enjoy it," Jason put in.

They smiled in their conspiracy. Actually, their Papa was such a descriptive storyteller; they honestly enjoyed hearing his tales again and again.

"Well, it <u>wus</u> an excitin' time," Gus began. His intense blue eyes began to light up, dancing, as he spoke.

"It wus a hot, dusty day in September, 1893. I left your Mama and the little lads Ben and Tom with my own mother in Virginee. Several of us came in days a'fore the race, to ride around and decide which tracts of land seemed the best. That way, we'd have somewhere in partic'olar to ride when we started."

"Mind you, we wern't like those danged 'Sooners' who went out and staked ahead of time; me and Clyfford Patrick, a friend o' mine, just rode around and looked things over! We stayed overnight in the dirty little hotel of a town within a mile of the border, several of us in one room." He paused.

"Next day, trains, packed so full that men wus riding on the roofs of cars and hangin' onto the sides pulled in for settlers to claim territory. I wus told that more'in 100,000 people scrambled for free land…

The race wus undescribable! People and wagons, schooners, stages, buggies, trains -- lined up *forever* on the Kansas border. Some even on bicycles and foot! Out in front wus soldiers, restin' easy on their rifles, chewing over the line. I wondered how they would manage to dodge the onrush. Horses got more and more restless and excitement pulsed to a high pitch way a'fore the cavalry gunshots to start at noon. When the sound exploded, so did the race! Horses wus a runnin' at break-neck speed; not long after … wagons overturned and some poor, pitiful people was trampled in the hot, dusty roar! But many of us just kept on a'ridin'."

"Gosh, it all sounds so exciting, Papa! I wish I could have

experienced it!" Jessie truthfully exclaimed. "A real adventure, right?"

Gus nodded.

"And you got this nice portion of land and have done really well for your trouble. Built us a fine home here, right, Papa?"

"Yes, Darlin', we done all right. It wus hard, 'specially on your Mother, but we worked hard and made a go of it. My own dear Mama came to live with us and helped us, too, God rest her soul. I can still picture her in her apron and bonnet, collectin' eggs, milkin' Whitey; out hoein' the garden, singin' whilst workin' the land. And cannin' ever' little bit o' thing she could get outta that dirt."

"Yes, she was one-of-a-kind, Papa; I still miss her so," Jessie agreed. "I don't know anyone I admired more than Grandmother McCarey. She had a true pioneer spirit, and Mama does, too."

Jessie looked lovingly over across the room at Mama and Kathleen smiled. Their mother had been quietly working, intent on her embroidery spreading roses on a pillowcase.

The boys all started looking at each other in amazement; they began to see where she was leading with this.

Jessie looked longingly at her father: "You know, Papa, a good adventure is always worth going after, don't you agree?"

He nodded his agreement.

"And you know I'm never one to want to miss out on any action … right, Papa?"

Gus patted her hand. "No, Darlin', you never want to miss out and I love you for your spirit."

"Well, I'm glad to hear that, because the boys and I want to tell you about a sort of bold little adventure of our own. And just like you did, we want to grab the opportunity at the best time."

Kathleen looked up from her work, questioningly, at Jessie.

"What are you mean'in, Jessie?" Gus asked.

"Well, we know that a lot of drilling for oil is going on right now, especially here in Oklahoma and like down at Spindletop, Texas. And we'd like to try some drilling on our own. *Right, Ben*?"

"Yes, Sir, we think we can make some real money drilling for oil," Ben quickly confirmed.

Their father grew thoughtfully silent. Jessie noticed their mother looked back and forth at all their faces with a worried expression, though she didn't say anything.

Stephen added, "Yeah, Papa, we're getting investors to help with the money, already have a lease on a spot we want to try, and hired a driller to start work as soon as we want to!"

Gus answered, "Sounds pretty loony to me, pokin' holes in the ground."

Jessie spoke up: "But Papa, there will be a big market for oil - they're coming up with more uses every day."

"Yes and we need to get started now, before all the good areas are used up," Stephen added.

"Ain't it a big gamble? Speculatin'? There's no guaranteein' you'll hit oil."

"We realize that, Papa, and as we get investors involved, we'll be frank with them, right up-front. But sometimes you just have to gamble, particularly when starting a business. And remember, *you* gambled when you came to Indian territory," Jessie reminded.

"So, you got this all figer'ed out. When ya plannin' to start?"

"Next week, actually. We should have a rig put together in a few days," Ben answered.

"How long have you been plannin' all this?" Gus asked.

"A few weeks," Jessie answered.

"That long? And you haven't mentioned it to your old Papa?"

"We didn't know for sure if we'd be able to get everything to work out; didn't want to get the rest of the family excited until we knew how to begin," Stephen explained.

"And now you're ready?"

"Yes, Sir, we think we are." Ben answered resolutely.

"What about the ranch? I need ya some around here."

"We figur'd you'd be worried 'bout that," Tom jumped in, "and we're all gonna keep working here at the ranch, too, 'specially me and Josh. Me and him will only be helpin' out at the drillin' site part of the time. I'm still not sure about this whole deal, anyway, but if the others want to give it a go, I won't get in their way. Josh and me will be here most of the time to help you, Papa."

"This can be a real adventure for us, Papa, but it's important to us that you approve," Jessie pleaded. "Please give us your blessing."

Gus looked tenderly at his daughter, then over at his wife. Kathleen shook her head, back and forth: *I don't like this.* He hesitated for some time, but in spite of Kathleen's negative reaction finally responded, "If you got your own money and think you can do it, go ahead. I'll not try t'stop ya."

Jessie looked around as they all breathed a sigh of relief -- for now.

-∞-

A few days later, Ben, Tom and Jason completed building the platform for the rig. It sat over on Samm Mann's property, waiting for work to begin. Jessie met again with the driller – a fella named Simpson Whiting, recommended to them by Roger Clayton, Jessie's close school friend. Good-natured, but ornery Roger felt like another brother to her. Jessie trusted Roger's judgment, so she felt confident Mr. Whiting would do a good job for them.

Sim Whiting was still hesitant about discussing business details with Jessie. Ben convincingly argued that Jessie knew what she was doing, so she was in charge of their family's interest.

When Sim learned that several members of the family wanted to work on the rig, he wasn't pleased about that, either. He'd told them it could cause problems. Jessie assured Sim that the boys all were strong, reliable and worked well together. She accepted that they would all have to take orders from Sim, herself included. Because of Sim's experience, Jessie emphasized that the family would definitely defer to his judgment. After talking awhile, he became more confident of her business-sense, so he relaxed somewhat.

Whiting mentioned hiring of a few more hands. Because of the living conditions in the area and the harshness of the work, he told Jessie they would probably have to hire some rough and colorful characters. "They're a breed apart. He..ck, some might even be outlaws." He explained that he usually didn't ask prospective hands much, except to find out what they could handle.

Sim knew that most of the men he hired would be accustomed to the 'rag towns' that had grown up overnight. Those places were so wild; people who had never experienced a boom town would never believe it. As Sim narrated lively incidents of girls-for-hire, fighting, theft, and a lot of bootleg drinking going on, Jessie chuckled.

He described the appalling living conditions -- walls of hotels so thin and thrown together, they held back little of the cold. Rooms were usually furnished only with old mattresses, nails driven in for hangers and perhaps a piece of looking-glass to shave. Most had a shared wash pan, a towel, a bar of lye soap, and a pail of water with a shared dipper. The toilet -- usually a double-dipper hole in the back yard. So the men would likely be rough.

Ben gave him a free reign to hire whomever he felt could do the best job and offered military-styled beds for Sim's crew in their bunkhouse. Since the ranch struggled financially, their Papa hadn't hired any extra hands to work the horses in the last couple of years. It would be a little crowded, but at least it was clean, with a privy out back and a tub for bathing. Sim seemed genuinely impressed with the offer: "Much better than the men are used to; they should appreciate it."

After discussing wages, Sim told them that he would see them at the site first thing Monday morning.

-∞-

As the day dawned for the drilling to begin, Jessie was beside herself with excitement. She woke early, way before dawn. Before the others rose, she skipped down the stairs to fetch water to start coffee brewing. She hopped out the back door of the kitchen and vigorously pumped enough water from the cistern to fill all the cooking pots. Shortly, her mother came into the kitchen, twisting her hair up in a bun on the back of her neck with long hairpins.

"What would you like me to do, Mama?" Jessie asked.

Her mother looked hard at her before answering, "Actually, Sarah, I'd like you to stay home with me today, but I suppose that's out of the question."

"Mama, don't be upset or worried by this. I'm not going to do any of the heavy work - that's the boys' job - but I need to keep the financial records organized. I know you don't understand my interest, but please try to accept that I need different things in my life than you do. This is important to me."

"I'll try, dear," Kathleen sighed, "but I don't know if I'll ever …"

Jessie excitedly hugged Kathleen. "Thank you, Mama, all I ask is that you just *try* to understand."

-∞-

Her brothers quickly ate breakfast and loaded supplies into their wagon. Jessie jumped up next to Ben and he reined up the horses.

Reaching Samm's property, they found Mr. Whiting awaiting them with four other men. Jessie was pleased to see one she knew: a large-framed black man -- Tyrone Jones, the good-natured brother of her friend, Maggie.

The Jones family lived a few miles from the McCarey homestead, across the wide pasture and a swirling creek. Jessie often incurred hostility because of her friendship with Maggie, but true to character, stubbornly refused to allow people to dissuade her. She'd done her best to bring Maggie books from school. But one day heading to Maggie's home, a couple of angry young men snatched them away from her. She'd had to retrieve them from the creek and carefully lay them out in the sun to dry, continually pulling apart the pages with a patient, gentle hand. In spite of the difficulties, Jessie doggedly enabled Maggie to learn to read a bit.

Jessie smiled and waved over to Tyrone. "Good to see you. How's Maggie?"

A big grin sprouted across Tyrone's huge bear of a face: She be jest fine, Mis Jessie, thankee for askin'."

Jessie's impression of the men: they looked pretty rough around the edges. *Good! They should be able to work hard.*

The men eyed *her* with a combination of appraisal, interest and suspicion. "*She* gonna be hangin' round here?" the one with stringy dirty blond-colored hair falling across his eyes asked roughly.

"You got that right, Pete, she is. And what she and Mr. Ben

McCarey here says, *goes*, you got that?" Sim was already annoyed at Pete Ware as Pete quickly griped about having to work with a black man. If he wasn't known to be such an adept hand with the equipment, Sim wouldn't have hired Pete at all. He just hoped the hard-head wouldn't be too much trouble.

"Yeah, well this ought'ta be interestin'," Pete mumbled. He turned to the other man and winked. They clustered together with some others, snickering vehemently about *this black-loving family*.

"Let's get to work!!" Sim yelled.

At Tom's direction, the workers slowly set up the substantial sides of the rig, anchoring it with cross-bars. Then, all the men joined in to haul the cable up to the suspension at the top of the rig.

When they completed the rig, the equipment appeared large and enormously heavy (and therefore dangerous) to Jessie. The drill was a huge, flat metal thing that looked like a giant's shovel on the end. Attached to a colossal metal rod about three feet in diameter and fifteen feet long, it suspended from a brace on the wooden rig tower.

Later that day, Jessie held her breath as she watched the first up-and-down motion of the lever, like a lance thrown against the rock, causing the bit to pound the ground and chip away the sedimentary rock. They were actually drilling! *What an exciting day for the McCarey family*!

-∞-

The drilling proceeded for several days without incident. Everyone worked hard, including Jessie. Drilling had to be interrupted periodically to remove loose rock chips with a basket-like thing on the cable. Because Jessie wasn't able to do the heavy lifting or straining, she tirelessly carried individual buckets of dirt and rock away from the hole, ran errands, brought food for the men, and generally helped out with whatever she could do. She labored over detailed notes in a journal every day about their progress so they would have accurate reporting to their investors.

Jessie cut down her time at Mr. McPherson's office to one day every other week, but between that, helping her mother at home, and working on the lease, Jessie dropped into her bed each night, exhausted, but exhilarated. *Gosh, she loved the work!* She couldn't begin to explain it -- just hoped the others felt the same.

| CHAPTER FOUR |

About three weeks into the drilling while the family's crew was fully engaged 'pulling' the drilling bit, Daniel Morgan dropped by the site. Daniel scrutinized the situation, unseen from the side for some time, before approaching Jessie. Hauling away a bucket of dirt, she looked really hot and dirty. From his stance, he appeared obviously displeased with her appearance and particularly that she was the only woman around.

Finally, he strode over to Jessie, tapping her shoulder: "I'd like to talk to you - over there." He jerked his head and pointed to a tree a short distance away from the others.

Jessie turned and beamed up at him. "Hey there! Did you come to see our operation? I'm so glad you stopped by."

"Actually, I came by to see what *you* are up to, since you haven't had time to see me for weeks …"

"I'm sorry, Danny, but we've really been swamped with work. I've been meeting myself coming and going working in town, at home and out here, too."

"Just what exactly are you doing out here?"

"I would think that's obvious - I'm working."

"I can see you're *working*, but what I want to know is, why?"

"Danny, you must know that we're operating here on a shoe-string, so *all* of us have to help out. Hopefully, if we strike oil, we'll have some revenue coming in and things won't be so tight financially. When that happens, I'll only have to oversee the work and keep the books."

"Oversee the work? Why can't you let Ben take care of that!?"

"Because this is my business; I want to keep my hands in what's going on. You know me - I relish learning and trying new things. This is like an adventure to me."

"Yeah, well, you're always getting into things you shouldn't be. Why can't you just stay home and do the normal things a woman does - like help your mother?! I don't think it looks good for you to be out here with all these men!"

Her brothers glanced in the direction where Jessie and Daniel were talking - or rather, Daniel yelling. They couldn't hear the conversation too well, but had a good guess of what was transpiring. The boys shook their heads, each thinking in their own way: *Daniel sounds like he's about to push Jessie into a very volatile mood, which won't be advantageous for him.* Jason grinned and winked at Ben, who shook his head and went back to work.

Secretly, Ben hoped Jessie would quit seeing Daniel Morgan. Ben was of the opinion that Daniel thought himself better than most other people, because he was the banker's son and well off. Ben appreciated people for their good qualities; wasn't impressed by how rich they were. To Ben, character was everything.

He'd stayed out of Jessie's private business -- *Jessie must see something worthwhile in Morgan.* After their night together in that barn ... and apparently Daniel hadn't tried too hard to have his way with her, [otherwise, Ben would'a had to kill him] ... well, Ben had to begrudgingly admit: *perhaps the guy genuinely cares for our sister.* His thoughts were broken by a rise in the pitch of Jessie's voice.

"You don't think it 'looks good'? You don't think it *'looks good'*!! Well, I don't give a flip how you think it looks! I've got work to do and I plan on doing it. If you can't speak to me in a civil tongue, then leave!"

Daniel's voice took on a dangerous tone: "If I leave, I won't be seeing you again, Jessie. I wish you'd go on home and think about this."

Jessie hesitated. She looked at Daniel for a curiously long time, as if she were seeing him for the first time. Finally: "There's nothing to think about, Danny. This is something exciting for me and I won't change my mind. If you can't deal with it, then perhaps we don't have anything worthwhile between us."

"So that's it, just like that?"

She took a deep, deliberate breath to calm down, and then answered: "*You're* the one forcing me to decide - you shouldn't make me choose between you and having a life. I'm not going to stay at home and spend my entire life washing dishes and scrubbing floors. I know that's important work - and I help Mama as much as I can, but there are other experiences I want to explore. I've got to have a life of my own."

"Well, if that's the way you feel, I guess we're through. I want a wife that will stay at home and help me with a family."

"A wife? You've never said anything to me about marriage."

"I figured you knew. I thought we understood each other."

Jessie hesitated. Finally she answered: "Obviously not, if you think I'd sit at home with no outside life."

"You'd have a great life – I'll need you to help entertain clients … important clients …"

"What … a waitress? Do you think that's what I am? That's just not what I want. I wish you'd cared enough to get to know me before you started planning my life."

"I thought you were an intelligent woman. Guess that's my mistake -- I thought I did know you."

"Obviously, you don't understand me at all. When did you take the time to discuss this with me? I have to tell you, marriage is the furthest thing from my mind for a while -- I've got a business to run."

"You've got to be kidding!! Women can't wait to get their hooks in a man. *All* women scheme to get married!" he growled.

Jessie could see this conversation was leading nowhere. She slowly and deliberately responded: "Not all. Goodbye, Danny."

She calmly turned and started back to work. Daniel, furiously red-faced, stared for some time; then got on his horse. The others all watched as he lingered a moment, but Jessie never turned back to acknowledge him. Finally, he violently spurred his poor horse and rode off.

Ben and Jason grinned smugly at each other.

-∞-

Shortly thereafter, Jessie had her first problem with the men at the rig. For the most part, the hands had begrudgingly admired her perseverance and endurance working tirelessly around the well. However, skinny, wiry Pete Ware began to make unwanted gestures and insinuations toward her, when he noticed her brothers weren't close by. He became especially fond of playfully tugging at the buttons on the front of her shirt.

She tried reasoning with him: "Pete, don't do that – we have to work together. This is distracting for everyone and we can't afford it -- we're on a tight budget and schedule."

But he stubbornly continued; egged on by the other man he hung out with. They laughed and elbowed each other, mocking her, until Pete finally got bold enough to grab Jessie and try to get his hands up her under her shirt. He snickered: "Come on, sweet little honey, gimme a little kiss - I bets ya really knows how to treat a man."

Jessie shoved him off and slapped him, *hard*. "Pete, I'm not going to put up with that, do you understand? So make up your mind if you want to work here …"

Jessie stomped over to the water bucket to get a drink and calm down. Pete and a few of the others continued laughing and making jokes about her figure and snide remarks about what all they'd like to do to her. Jessie ignored them, thinking they'd eventually tire of their game and leave her alone.

However, Tom heard part of what transpired and strode over to tell Ben and Jason: "I *knew* this would happen, having her out here! Can't believe it hasn't already. What are we gonna do?"

Ben sat, silent for a moment, then replied: "We're not going to do anything, as long as she seems to be handling it."

"Not *do* anything? It's only gonna get worse. This is no place for a woman!"

Ben retorted: "And just what do you think we should do about it? If we fire those men, we won't be able to keep up a crew."

"I wasn't talking about firin' the men," Tom replied quietly. "I think we should send Jessie home, where she belongs."

"And just how do you propose we do that? *If* you will remember correctly, this operation is Jessie's. She did all the leg work and is completely responsible for starting what's goin' on out here. As long as she can handle it, I think we should support her."

"Support her, he--!"

Jason interrupted: "Tom, you 'member that hunt'in trip Papa took y'all on two years ago, up north?"

"Yeah, what has that got to do with this?" he demanded.

"Well, if ya think back, Jessie wanted to go real bad. But for once, Papa told her no; that he didn't think it was the kinda trip she should be on."

"And...?" Tom asked impatiently.

"Well, ya know as well the rest of us that Jessie can sit a horse for days, and she's as good a shot as eny of us. Jess would make a heck of a hunter, given half a chance. She wanted to go on that trip so bad, I felt guilty I turned it down."

"So?"

"So … after you all left, she wander'd around the stable, real quiet-like and I followed after her, somewhat behind. Then she went down to'ard the creek and I wus worried, so I snuck down after her. When I got close'nuff to see her, she wus sobbing so hard, it shook 'er body. Man, it 'bout killed me to watch how sad she was! Went on for maybe half-hour! I wus sure she'd be sick."

"So, she felt sorry for herself and had a good bawling spell. Women do it all the time."

"Not like 'at, they don't. She wus so disappointed, it scared me. If you'da seen er, you'd understand. Anyway, she didn't pout and act up about it like a baby. She had a good cry, then splashed her face with water in the creek and headed back home. She went in and helped Mama with the warshin' the rest of the day. Can you 'magine bein' the only girl in the family? Expectd to do warsh'in and iron'in all day, rather than bein' outside enjoyin' the countryside? Made me awful glad to be a man, ya know? *I'd* hate to be stuck with that kinda life, wouldn't you…? Think about it!"

Tom grew thoughtful as he faced Ben and the others. Frustrated, he stared over where Jessie busily jotted notes. She glanced up and smiled at him.

"Well, maybe I am a little hard on 'er, but you know, *she's* kinda hard to take sometimes."

They all nodded in agreement and, laughing, slapped him on the back. Ben nodded, hinting in Jessie's direction.

Getting the clue, Tom ambled toward Jessie, who was taking a needed break with a drink of cool water. "Jess, I heard what happened earlier. You okay?"

"I'm fine, Tom, don't be concerned about me ... [she looked up at his worried expression] -- *really.* I can handle the likes of Pete Ware. You remember that shiner I gave Jason when we were about the same size? If Pete tries that again, I'm going to *punch his lights out!*"

He smiled down at the way her cute little nose wrinkled up -- the sweet gesture of a little girl. "Yeah, I sup'ose you can. But if you find yourself need'in a hand, you let me know, okay?"

"Thanks, Tommie, I will." Then she looked up at him with such a tenderness, he was forced to turn away before she saw the emotional turmoil in his face.

-∞-

About two weeks into the work, Jessie and Ben critically studied her logging reports. They'd reached a depth that exceeded what Sim felt reasonable for continuing the drilling. Sim told them he thought they might be 'throwing good money after bad.' Jessie asked Sim to have the crew continue for a couple more days. If they hadn't hit oil by then, they would discuss moving the drilling equipment and trying a new site before their funds ran out.

Ben looked worried, so Jessie admonished: "Cheer up, Big Bubba; we knew this wasn't going to be easy! Besides, Tom noticed a rainbow sheen on the creek yesterday ... a sure sign of some kind of oily stuff around here."

"I know, Jess; I need more of your optimism. I just worry about the money and ..."

He glanced over where one of the explosives shooters built a fire by whittling and burning sticks of dynamite. She followed his look and laughed out loud when he moaned.

"Makes it kinda excitin', right?" she teasingly drawled.

"Oh yeah ... oh yeah, ... I just *luv* some of the stunts these guys pull. Can't wait to see what they come up with next!"

Ben wearily resumed work and Jessie continued writing her notes.

During a later rest break, Jessie noticed Pete Ware stroll over to the area where they'd stored dynamite and sat down. Some of the others were off at a distance, smoking. Resting in the shade a further distance away, Ben and his brothers languished propped up against the supply wagon.

Jessie noticed one of the hands throw down his cigarette and soon after, a thin trail of fire licked down the pasture. She wondered if someone had spilled some powder there, or something else flammable. It suddenly occurred to her that the fire could spread down toward the dynamite. She yelled at Pete, but he was too far away to hear her. She waved and signaled to her brothers. Determining they were even further away from Pete than she was, Jessie took off running toward Pete.

Tyrone spied Jessie frantically running and yelling, waving her arms toward Pete. Quickly sizing up what was happening with the fire, he took off at a dead run toward her. Because of his height and leg strength, Tyrone easily overtook Jessie; rather than waste time haggling with her, he shoved her to the ground, sprinting on toward Pete.

Pete finally looked up, but still hadn't caught sight of the spreading trail of fire, so didn't understand what Jessie had been signaling. Tyrone grabbed Pete, and, pointing to the spreading flames, ran with him in the opposite direction, where they flung themselves into a ravine.

Ben, Jessie and the others began running back. Finally discerning the problem, they also dove to the ground, covering their heads with their hands in preparation for an explosion. In a few seconds, the fire reached the dynamite and the expected, but still-terrifying noise resonated. The wooden shed housing the explosives *burst* into splinters, dirt spewing everywhere!

As soon as the dust started settling, everyone grabbed gunny sacks, beating at the fire, hoping to stop it before it could spread to the well. Finally, the fire extinguished; each dropped where they stood, exhausted.

Once he regained his breath, Ben screamed: "I've had about enough of this loose attitude around here! No one seems to think safety is important, but it will be now! *Anything* explosive will be stored properly! And smoking will only be done far enough away from operations that we say is safe for smoking, ya'll got that?!!"

Everyone quietly nodded -- they seemed pretty much still in shock.

Jessie spoke up: "Pete, that was an especially close scare for you. Don't you think you should thank Tyrone for saving your life?"

Pete sulked off: "Yeah, *whatever*."

Jessie added: "He risked his own life to help you. He didn't have to do that. I think you should shake his hand and thank him like a gentleman."

"Oh ya do, do ya? And just what'll ya do if'in I don't? Ya gonna *fire* me, *'Boss Lady'*?" Pete sneered.

Jessie hesitated, and then looked squarely at Pete. "No, I'm not stupid. I *could* fire you, but I won't. You're too good a hand, Pete. I just won't have any respect for you, that's all."

Pete looked around at the others; when most shrugged their shoulders, he glanced back at Jessie. He remembered seeing her frantically waving and running toward him before Tyrone had reached her. Pete had to know she risked herself for him, until Tyrone intervened. He gradually walked over to Tyrone.

"Thanks for what ya did." Pete slowly, reluctantly, stuck out his right hand.

Tyrone hesitantly stared at Pete, and then extended his. "It's okay, man. I done it for Jessie."

The others smiled their approval, until Sim yelled cheerily, "Back to work, you slackers!"

Things went pretty peaceful for the next few days - the atmosphere seemed to be more cooperative and friendly. Tyrone finally warmed somewhat to Pete – and, unbelievably, vice versa.

-∞-

Two days later, as everyone labored, an unexpected rumble reverberated from the ground. Suddenly, an explosive *roar* erupted that sounded something like … a tornado and a train mixed together.

Each looked around at each other, as oil came *gushing* out of the derrick! Quickly, the immediate area and the workers were covered with a fine mist of black stuff.

Jessie screamed maniacally, jumping up and down. She ran to Ben, threw her arms around his neck and they danced like crazy people, round and round the rig.

She hugged each of her brothers, as Jason and Josh did a mock Indian war whoop. They kept yelling: "We're gonna be rich ... we're gonna be rich!"

"Doesn't this stuff smell won-der-ful!??" she joked.

The other workers joined in the celebration. Tom uncorked a bottle of mash from the wagon and offered everyone a toast. They all poked fun of each other, especially Jessie, covered and grimy with the black liquid all over her hair and face. She laughed along, oblivious to the greasy oil - she thought it the loveliest stuff she'd ever seen!

As soon as they regained their composure, Sim and Tom yelled: "Grab those fittings! We've got to try and get this thing slowed down!" They began to instruct the workers on how to choke the exploding black gold.

-∞-

Later, Ben and Tom thrashed out methods of loading the oil to transport it to buyers. A friend had earlier suggested some contacts, so the first obstacle: how to store and ship it.

The next few days were spent containing their prize. Tom had earlier recommended nine-inch diameter wooden pipe to move the crude from the working well to a large storage tank. The oil slowly soaked into the wooden pipe, preserving it and causing it to swell, which sealed the joints connecting the eight-foot sections. Soon, much of their prize was loaded in large wooden barrels and they were ready to ship to buyers Stephen had earlier contacted.

Jessie sounded out Ben: "While you and Tom figure out the logistics of the supply, we really need to find some office space in Big Spring. I've been talking with Mr. McPherson about what we might do to become a company, perhaps a corporation, and maybe put shares of the business on the open market. Get more investors to spread around the risk of our working capital. Why don't I go into town and do some preliminary search for a location?"

"Sure, you handle all the bookwork and details, Jess – we'll worry about the operations out here."

"Okay, I've got another idea, too; I've been meaning to sound you out about."

"What's that?"

"Hiring Roger Clayton to work with us. Now that we've got something to sell, we need to accurately account for everything – some better bookkeeping system for company assets, taxes and sales. Roger would be the best person to help us with this - he's familiar with the oil business from working with his cousins last summer."

"You know, Jess, one producing well doesn't make a company."

"Yes, but I believe this is just the first of many. We're on our way, now, Ben, I just feel it!"

| CHAPTER FIVE |

Within a few days Jessie rented cheap space in an old building in Big Spring. Soon it gained the appearance of an office - although pretty rough-looking: wooden crates for desks and chairs, but that was all right; like Ben, she didn't want to spend money too quickly.

She easily persuaded Roger Clayton into joining them and the two busily set up contracts and invoices with buyers, and worked on procedures to account for and transport the crude oil. They daily poured over logging reports, expenses, all kinds of invoices and papers.

Roger suggested they propose a drilling contract with Willie Smithsom, who owned some of the adjoining property to the Mann's place. That would prevent other wildcatters depleting the reservoir they'd discovered. Jessie agreed that would be a better legal asset than just a stay lease. Though Mr. Smith didn't have money to drill, if they didn't get that option, someone else would quickly buy it from him.

One evening after a hard day's work Jessie confided: "Rog, this is so great - us working together. It's like the good old times at school! Remember helping me with my math? I'd never have passed without you."

Roger agreed with a smile: "It is great, Jess. And ... don't give me too much credit -- you paid me back, writing those danged essays. Man, I hated all that English stuff; but it just seemed natural for you – you knocked out those papers in record time. I'm glad you invited me in on this – it's a great opportunity."

"Do you suppose … in case we go belly-up," Jessie asked hesitantly, "… that the Townsends would give you back your old job?"

"Well, you never know, but they can't seem to find anyone who enjoys bookkeeping, so would probably be glad to have me back. If not, I'll find something else – Big Spring is booming."

"Good! I'm feeling a bit guilty. But you were the *only* choice for this job, Roger. I've always admired what a good head you have for figures."

Roger looked wistfully at her. For some crazy reason, he could never bring himself to say so, but thought: *I wish that wasn't all you admired.*

Jessie beamed at him as they closed up the office for the evening. Roger had to smile back. He could never be sore at her; no matter how disappointed he felt. She was like a best friend.

He could kick himself for not letting her know how he felt earlier. Roger just sensed he couldn't compete with the likes of that banker's son. When he'd heard they'd broken up, he was initially ecstatic, but couldn't believe Daniel Morgan wouldn't be back after his temper cooled off -- *she was special*. If she didn't make up with Morgan, Roger clung to the hope that sometime she might notice *him* for more than just a platonic friend.

-∞-

Jessie's hunches proved right. The next nine wells the family drilled came in before they ever struck a dry hole. The company suddenly looked very prosperous.

As Ben, Jessie and Roger grew more and more involved in the administrative work at the office, Tom and Jason watched over most of the operations at the sites.

Once they were financially able, Jessie promised to hire a foreman to oversee the drilling work. Then, Tom would be able to return to the ranch (his real love) to help their father. Jason, quickly becoming quite the businessman, would assume drilling decisions along with their foreman.

All along, Josh and Matt spent most of their time at the ranch, as sales of horse stock, surprisingly, began to increase.

Stephen worked at the rig through the summer, and then headed off to law school. It was satisfying that the family could help with his tuition and Stephen could fully concentrate on school rather than the expenses.

Roger was continually impressed with Jessie's growing knowledge of the oil business. Not only did she quickly comprehend the financial statements he prepared for her, but he often marveled at her discussions with Ben, Tom and others about faults, traps, porosity, specific gravity, geology, etc. All he could think, as usual: *what a woman*!

In spite of Ben's misgivings, within a few months Jessie, Roger and Mr. McPherson completed the paperwork for incorporation of *McCarey Oil Company* - registered in Delaware with Ben as President.

Jessie knew it would be best for now if she appeared as Ben's behind-the-scenes 'assistant.' Remembering how hard it had been to convince Sim of her ability, he finally agreed it would probably be easier that way, rather than Jessie needing to force her authority on customers, employees, etc.

It bothered Ben that he'd be getting the attention for their success, but Jessie assured him she was content (as long as he respected her judgment and involved her in the decision-making.)

"Ben, I'm realistic about what I can do. I've heard of women getting whipped for even asking their fathers or husbands about business or things like voting. Doesn't matter what the legal papers state. We're partners; that's the way it'll always be."

"I could never have done this without you, Jess, believe me," he assured her often.

-∞-

Jessie was relieved the family was doing well financially. Soon, she and Ben agreed they could spend less time at the rig. They hoped their family could take turns working on Sundays, so each could get back to attending worship services. The drilling never shut down, so they committed to hire more hands and rotate daily assignments. Fully knowing it probably wasn't a priority for most of the roughnecks, but that way, the others could attend if they wished.

Jessie knew Pastor Murphy was concerned about their absences. He often came to the site on Sunday afternoons for Bible study during the employees' breaks. Though she gave their dedicated, good-natured pastor a bad time, she honestly wouldn't impede him. Oklahoma was still so wild; *a little moral influence couldn't hurt any of them.* She wouldn't push religion on the men; that was their call. And besides, Pastor Murphy was such a good man -- funny and witty; the workers just naturally responded to him.

-∞-

Their parents, especially Gus, were enormously proud of their children. Gus knew some gambles were worth taking and this one was paying off.

He often thought to himself: *McCarey Oil! McCarey Oil Company!* He just couldn't believe it -- what a legacy. Gus wistfully yearned that his own Father, their rock who had slaved in the coal mines to feed his large family, could have lived to see his grandchildren's success.

But the McCarey brood's Papa was far too hard on himself. Gus should have realized his Father would have been proud of *his* bold adventure: the scary move to homestead in Oklahoma. And more importantly: that Gus and Kathleen were raising such a gutsy, yet honest family. The McCarey family had the kind of trustworthy reputation and respect that people envied -- something not bought with money.

| CHAPTER SIX |

Tom completed his errands in Big Spring and decided he sure could use a cool drink. He debated about a soda over at Jeremiah's store, but finally thinking: *what the heck*, surrendered to a beer at Clinton's Tavern. Sitting at the bar, he began to reminisce about the last time he'd been in here -- the day Ben and Stephen brought Jessie inside this dump.

Tom glanced around, almost as if to check to make sure Jessie wasn't here again. Guessing his mind, the bartender jokingly asked, "Whatcha doin'? Lookin' for your little sister?"

"Who knows? What a pain in the butt she can be sometimes!"

The bartender laughed and brought him another glass of beer. "Tom, she ain't been back in here, so don't worrie. That day <u>wus</u> fun -- she give us all somethin' to talk 'bout, eny how. We gotta real kick outta her."

Still grimacing at the thought of Jessie's antics, Tom felt a tap on his shoulder and turned to find a tall, dark-headed man grinning crazily at him. Tom studied the man a moment before recognition spread across his face.

"Jake, Jake Trenton! What in the world are you doing in Big Spring?!!"

Tom grabbed the man's hand and pumped it heartily, all the while vigorously slapping Jake's back with his free hand. Tom was thrilled to see the friend he connected with working for Uncle Duke in Pennsylvania a few years back. Though the two had become fast friends, Tom never dreamed he'd see Jake again.

Jake continued to smile at Tom. "I kept hearing about all the hub-bub going on down in Indian territory so I decided to come to Oklahoma and see for myself. What luck! I just got into town and was about to ask where I might find you, when lo and behold, I see you're sitting right there."

"You gonna be here long?"

"That depends. I'm trying to drum up some business in this area. Sick of the hassle back east and thought I might try my luck elsewhere."

"What kind of business you look'in for?"

"Well, I finally got my pilot's license and financed a small plane. I want to do some delivery work, barnstorming, crop-dusting … whatever I can find."

Tom smiled again while asking: "So you went and learned to fly, did ya? I figured that was a just a pipe-dream without your Papa's money."

"It was tough, especially not taking anything from Father to do it. I worked hard and saved the money myself. Finally attended that school the Wright brothers set up. There are only a few registered pilots right now in the whole country and I'm one of the few!"

"That's great! Glad to hear it. I know a few folks around here; I'll recommend you. Hey, you won't believe it, but I'm kinda involved in a risky business myself right now," Tom said.

"Really? What are you doing?"

"My family's drillin' for oil. Just got started and already brought in several good wells. Hope'in for more. This seems to be a good area for it."

"Yeah," Jake replied. "I've been reading about the excitement of everything booming here in Oklahoma and Texas, and decided this might be a ripe area for opportunity. Let's have a drink and toast to successes for us both." Jake raised his glass and clinked against Tom's.

Tom was ecstatic about the thought of Jake doing business here in the area. He just couldn't believe it! Tom told Jake a bit about his family and asked Jake if he'd like to come out to the ranch for supper sometime to meet them -- he assured Jake his Mama would love to have him.

The invitation touched Jake. He told Tom "that would be really nice, perhaps in a few days." Then added, "I'll be busy for awhile, contacting those prospective customers you mentioned."

Tom finally asked, "Hey, what you doin' Saturday nite?"

"Probably busy hustling work every day, so will get a room at the local hotel and turn in early. Why? Anything special going on?"

Tom responded that there would be a big dance in town and lots of people from the area would be there, especially mentioning pretty girls. He said that his sister Jessie should be there, but no promises on getting a dance on her card. Jake hesitated, replying that he didn't know; he'd see how his schedule would be lining up later in the week.

Tom tempted, "Jake, can ya take a minute to ride out with me to one of the sites we're drilling? I'm finished for the day, just need to drop off some papers Ben asked me to pick up."

Jake responded that he would definitely be interested in seeing how the work was done but probably should settle in for the evening. " I want to make early contacts tomorrow."

"Aw, come on, Jake ... come *on*! You'll be back before dark. I can borrow a horse for you from a friend of mine down the street."

"Well ... okay, it's been such a long time since I've seen you, but remember: I can't stay late. I've got to start making a living."

"Won't take long and you can meet some of my brothers. They should still be at the rig. Let's go!"

-∞-

When they reached the site, Tom introduced Jake to Ben and explained that he'd invited Jake to see their operations. When Jake told Ben he didn't want to be in the way and would stand off to the side, watching, Ben reached out a bear-sized paw and squeezed Jake's hand. "Any friend of Tom's always welcome."

Ben politely took time to explain to Jake how the drilling was done – he described 'spudding-in,' cable tools, using mud for cooling the bit, etc. Always interested in learning new things, the operation impressed Jake.

Ben's attention to explaining the parts of the rig was distracted by murmurs of some of the other men. The men began looking out toward the road, so Ben, Tom and Jake followed their glances that direction.

Weaving across the dirt road at a good rate of speed, a Model-T furiously scattered dust. As the car bore down toward them, Ben thought that the driver would begin to slow down, but it kept coming at the same speed, directly at them. His crew looked anxiously at one another and jumped away from the car's path. About ten feet from them, seemingly at the very last moment, the car swerved around the rig and hurtled a ditch to the side, finally bumping to rest against a soft mound of spewing dirt.

Ben strode to the car, prepared to direct a few choice expletives at the driver, when Jessie jumped out, a smile stretching the width of her face.

"Hi, Ben, Jason's giving me driving lessons! Isn't it grand?! I already *love* driving!!"

Ben gave Jason a dark look as he exited the passenger's side. Jason sheepishly shrugged his shoulders, as if to say, *You try and stop her when she wants to do something.*

Jessie recognized the look and quickly rattled:

"Oh, Ben, don't lecture Jason; I kept at him until he agreed to teach me. After all, I'm sixteen months older than the twins, so I should be able to drive, too. It will be *so* useful and now I can more-quickly run errands for you, which you *know* will help out here on the rig. The steering's not too bad; but that 'shifting' and clutching is what I have to work on. What do you think of my first test drive - pretty good, right?!!"

Ben's dark glance faded into one of mild annoyance. The other workers began to laugh and joke around with Jessie.

"Well, Jess, I wouldn't exactly say you were ready for racing yet, but knowing you, you'll get it. I won't be surprised if perty soon you'll be wanting to compete with the likes of Ray Harroun at the Indy."

While she beamed up at Ben, excitedly chattering on, Jake's glance appreciatively took in the slim figure (in an old shirt and worn pair of … *looks like a cast-off pair of boys' trousers*), the windblown, shiny hair and the animated expression. Jake decided this trip was worth the time – here's a woman he'd like to get to know. But that must come later.

Before he could become further delayed with conversation, he turned toward the borrowed horse. Jake quickly asked, "What time did you say that dance starts Saturday night?"

Tom smiled as he responded: "It's still eight o'clock, like I told you. Did ya have a change of heart?"

"Believe I did - see you Saturday." He grinned as he got on the horse and rode off toward town.

-∞-

The weather on Saturday evening turned out to be the perfect complement for a dance. Open town hall windows enabled everyone to enjoy the cooler, evening breeze. Conversation buzzed loudly, young men shyly talking with pretty girls, youngsters playing and running in and out, older people in groups talking about the town growing, or the weather, crops, and the latest problems with the farming.

Oil workers, freshly scrubbed, admired the local girls. Streamers decorated the ceiling and ladies busily arranged punch and cookies on a long table. The band musicians organized their materials in the far corner. There an old patchwork quilt covered the solid stacks of bailed hay that would act as their platform. Fellas began strumming their guitars, preparing for the evening's entertainment.

The McCarey family all rode to town together in their wagon. Gus wasn't ready yet, for a drive in that new-fangled horseless buggy. Besides -- not enough room for everyone, anyway.

Gus slid his long legs over the side of the wagon and held his arms up to Kathleen. As she elegantly descended, he smiled proudly at how lovely she looked in a long, swirling white dress dotted with tiny blue flowers. She took his arm to enter the dance.

Ben helped Jessie down and as they strolled in, he told her she 'sure was pretty.' She'd brushed her light, coppery-gold hair till it lay in a soft, shiny pageboy at her shoulders. In her nicest frock: an off-the-shoulder style in a color that nearly matched the sea green of her eyes, Ben knew she'd get plenty of attention, as usual.

Sure enough, as soon as they entered, the Bradford twins eyed them and headed straight in the direction where they stood. Ben offered to get Jessie something to drink but she looked at him imploringly: *Please don't desert me here with these two.* The Bradford twins, a year younger, always stuck at Jessie's heels like little lost puppies. She liked them both, but they seemed so immature; she sometimes felt they were real pests.

Ben winked and said he'd be right back. Before he could return to Jessie with a cup of punch, he spied MaryBeth Stockton sitting with her family. Now Ben had been thinking of asking MaryBeth out for some time, but with so busy at the site; he'd scarcely had time for anything other than work. Looking back toward Jessie, he pointed toward MaryBeth.

Jessie smiled and silently mouthed '*O.K.*' to him. MaryBeth was Jessie's best friend and Jessie had schemed to fix them up for some time. Ecstatic, she watched Ben offer MaryBeth the glass of punch.

Tom was also pleased when Jake strolled in a little later. As they shook hands, Tom introduced him to the family members who were sitting nearby. Ben had already pretty much become enthralled with MaryBeth, and Jessie surrounded by fellows requesting dances. Like a sentry, Tom observed Daniel Morgan across the room, staring intensely at Jessie.

Jake noticed Tom's expression: "Trouble?"

"Not sure. Jilted ex-suitor."

Jake laughed.

Shortly, Daniel caught Jessie's eye and nodded politely. When Jessie smiled back, Tom relaxed and picked up two cups of punch. Tom then winked at Jake and indicated they should step outside the back door. There Tom poured a homemade concoction into their cups from a bottle in the wagon and the pair went back inside.

Jake watched Jessie off and on, most of the evening. He courteously requested dances from a few of the girls Tom introduced him to, but in between, scarcely took his eyes off Jessie. He noted that practically every single man in the place had either offered to get her a drink or asked her to dance, even an old man named Red Stephens, her current partner.

Quite the dancer for his age, probably about seventy-five, but still Red appeared a lively fellow. Jake found Jessie's animated demeanor and good-natured laughing at Red's jokes quite appealing. She seemed to be enjoying a break from the twins' over-attentiveness. Red swung Jessie around and around, so she was actually doing a lot more of the dancing than he was, her skirt and blazing copper hair spinning. She soon became flushed from their quick pace in the two-step music.

After she danced with several local boys and each of the twins a couple of times, Eli Bradford headed toward her again. Jake noted Jessie's grimace toward Tom: *Oh no, not <u>again</u>!*

Tom started across the room, but Jake tapped him on the arm and offered: "I'll handle this assignment." Tom chuckled and strolled over to a pretty brunette sitting alone.

Just as Eli asked Jessie for the next dance, Jake smoothly slid his hand under her arm and down toward her hand, clasping it in his.

"Sorry, fella, but I believe the lady promised this one to me." Eli seemed disappointed, but backed away in a gentlemanly manner.

Jessie looked up curiously at Jake, but allowed him to lead her onto the dance floor in a slow waltz. "I suppose I should introduce myself - my name's Jake Trenton."

Jessie scrutinized the tall, dark-headed man she danced with. She thought him rather good-looking, *maybe twenty-six, twenty seven ...?* "Oh...yes! You must be the friend of Tom's I've heard so much about. I'm pleased to meet you and especially appreciative of the rescue."

Jake smiled down at her upturned face. *Cute little nose, especially with those sunny freckles splattered across.* Not a classically beautiful face, but extremely pleasant to look at. He noticed a tiny crescent-shaped scar at the left side of her chin. *Wonder what mischief wrought that ...?*

He thought it refreshing that she smiled often and bet she was a very good sport. *Good-looking, smart and a pleasant personality*, he mused.

"My pleasure," he responded sincerely.

When Jessie asked him if he was enjoying his stay in Oklahoma, Jake responded that yes, he liked this part of the country. "The people are so friendly, and I'm excited at the prospect of finding some regular work here."

At the end of their dance Jessie looked back toward the side of the room where young men had vied for her attention all evening. The twins and several other young men were sitting or standing nearby, waiting. Jake discerned her glance and asked if she'd like to go outside for a walk. She said that she *was* a little warm from the dancing and would enjoy some air. Jake led her outside, amusedly aware of the disappointed sighs from across the room (including that of the apparently too-late-in-acting ex-beau …)

Walking a short distance from the building, they came upon a sturdy fence. In a comfortable manner, Jake put his hands at Jessie's waist and lifted her up to sit on one of the rails. He stood quietly next to her as they wordlessly enjoyed the clear night full of stars, a cool breeze and the faint strains of the music wafting from the town hall.

Finally, Jessie asked, "So you think you'll be able to do some flying here, Mr. Trenton?"

"It's *Jake*."

"Oh. Okay … Jake. You think you'll find work? Flying must be so exciting!"

"I've talked with some people here and in several other towns. I think I may be able to do some delivery runs for them. Could always do a little barn-storming and, if worse comes to worse, charge to take people up for rides. Yes, it's fantastic being up there, high above the world. Makes me feel so free. Would you like to go up with me sometime?"

"Really? Are you kidding? I'd love to! I ... just don't know when, though; I'm completely swamped with work lately."

"Yeah, I've heard about your family's operation. You sound like quite a little business woman. But maybe you can work in a *little* free time."

Jessie blushed at the compliment. "We're giving it a try -- I'm hopeful we'll be successful. We're incorporating the family business. I think it will be beneficial, especially having more investors to absorb some of the expense and responsibility."

"Sounds like you've planned where you're heading. That's a rare, admirable trait -- knowing what you want."

He smiled down into those mesmerizing eyes. Jessie blushed again and it confused her. Normally very self-assured with people, even men, but *this* man was having an unusual effect on her.

Jessie grew quiet. Neither spoke for some time, but they seemed comfortable enough together. Jake looked down at her face, content from the music playing faintly in the background. He could hear the romantic lyrics: "*How could I help ... falling in love ... with the prettiest girl in the county*" and was stirred with the thought of kissing her.

That charming pair of big green eyes mirrored the moonlight's illumination, seemingly beckoning to him. Her glance never wavered from his and before she knew it, his lips touched her soft, moist mouth; she closed her eyes. It began gently at first, and then he kissed her more and more urgently. He bent his head and slid his mouth slowly down her warm, smooth neck, wisps of soft hair caressing his face. Exhaling a warm sigh of contentment, her fingers instinctively reached up, stroking the hair at the nape of his neck.

When her upper body pressed closer toward him, he lifted her from the fence, experiencing a palpating rush of heat as the length of her slid down against him. *She smelled so good, a little like violets.* He kissed her again and again till they were both nearly breathless before he finally tore his mouth away from hers.

It took Jessie a moment to recover. She heard Jake say something about going back in with the others as he led her back toward the dance. To be perfectly honest, she was a little disappointed that he wanted to stop, but then chided herself for allowing a stranger to kiss her – and so intimately: *Shame on you, you hussy.* It was really curious, though, how trusting she felt with him; as if it was natural for them to act this way.

They lingered just outside the door and listened to sounds of the dance ending. People milled around, talking and laughing as they were leaving.

Jake whispered, "Looks like we timed that just right."

"Yes, I suppose so," Jessie answered wistfully.

He looked down intently at her and laughed softly. "Don't you think for a moment I'm through with you, Miss McCarey. I'll be around to see you soon. If that's okay with you …?"

"I'd like that."

They stealthily reentered the hall. When they'd located her family, Jake turned to her parents: "It was very nice meeting you, Ma'am, Sir."

"We're happy to meet the friend Tom's spoken so highly of," Kathleen said. Then added: "Come for supper sometime, Jacob."

"Thank you, Mrs. McCarey. I'd enjoy some home cooking."

"I see you've met Jake," Tom commented wryly in Jessie's direction as he approached the group.

Jake smiled. "Yes, and Jessie has agreed to come flying with me. I'll ride over next week to visit," he whispered purposefully to Jessie as he turned and strode toward the door.

"Just like that?" Tom teased, pleased for a change in Jessie's taste in a man.

"Yes, I suppose ... just like that."

| CHAPTER SEVEN |

The following Saturday found Jessie exhausted. By four o'clock, she headed for home, a bath and some sweet rest. A couple of miles before reaching the ranch in the car, she and Jason were intercepted by Jake Trenton on horseback.

"Hello, Jessie, I'm just on my way over to your place. Are you busy tonight?"

Jessie's first reaction: tell him that she was really tired, but instead found herself answering, "No, not particularly. I was heading home to take a bath and just relax." She glanced down at her filthy clothes. "As you can see, I'm in dire need of it!" She laughed at herself.

Jake smiled. "How about if I come over around seven o'clock and take you out for that ride in my plane? It's not too far away, about a quarter-hour by horseback from your house. It'll be light for quite awhile."

"I believe I'd enjoy that," she heard herself saying.

"Okay, see you at seven." He waved and rode off toward town.

Jessie turned and headed the car gingerly down the old trail toward home. "Too bad we don't have roads in here."

Jason cantankerously mimicked in a falsetto: "I thought you were '*so*' tired ... *home tonight for a bath and bed.*"

"Don't make me whack you, silly boy."

Actually, she wondered to herself why she had accepted Jake's invitation - she needed some sleep badly.

"Oh, well, maybe the bath will revive me!" She chuckled.

When she arrived home and into the tub, she found it indeed worked miracles. Changing into a clean riding skirt and a white cotton blouse, she felt relaxed and more energetic than she earlier thought she would. However, she might just take off work at the rig tomorrow. Because she'd worked some every single day for months, she figured they could do without her.

Jake arrived promptly at seven o'clock, clad in freshly-pressed pants and a nice blue shirt. As she answered the door, Jessie wondered to herself who ironed his clothes for him. She laughed at the thought - *as if it were any of my business. Maybe I'd rather not know.*

She took Jake's arm and led him into the kitchen, where most of the family still assembled, talking, after supper.

"You all remember Jake Trenton, don't you?"

They nodded and Tom came around to slap Jake on the back. What's happenin' with you two tonight? Got a date?"

"Yes, as a matter of fact, I came to take Jessie up in my plane this evening. It looks like a good time - not much wind tonight."

Kathleen looked anxiously at Jessie. Jessie immediately recognized the look, reassuring: "It's perfectly safe, Mama, lots of people are flying these days."

Before anyone else could object, Jessie quickly took Jake's arm, telling him they probably should be leaving. They walked outside, where he'd left his horse tied to a porch rail. When Jake noticed Tom standing nearby, he mounted the horse, then extended his hand to help Jessie on behind. Tom cupped his hands and gave her a boost up.

"I'll have her back home soon," he said to Tom and the twins, who'd followed them out to the porch.

"Have fun; next time it's my turn," grinned Josh.

"Me, too!" exclaimed Matthew.

"Sure, I'll take any of you up that would like to go. Anytime I'm not working," Jake promised.

They rode off toward the clearing where Jake kept his small plane. Jessie wrapped her arms around Jake's waist and enjoyed the rhythm of the horse moving beneath them. Soon, they reached the clearing and he helped her down from the horse.

When they climbed up into the plane, Jake asked: "You sure you're up for this?"

"You bet! Why do you ask?"

"Well, I've had people chicken-out on me before," Jake grinned.

"Not *this* little chick," Jessie teased back.

"Good girl."

Jake explained to Jessie about the instrumentation and principles behind flying the plane. He showed her the fuel-tank gauges, oil-pressure gauge, speed indicator and manifold-pressure gauge.

"This is the control lever -- we call it a 'stick.' Up and back movements of this stick move the elevators up and down and change pitch. Side to side movements change the position to produce roll. When coordinated together, these movements give the control necessary to make properly banked turns."

Jessie asked, "How does the plane stay up?"

"Good question. Here's a cram-course in aviation training: airplanes take off and climb because the propeller system produces a forward thrust greater than the combined ground and air resistance. The result of that forward motion makes air flow over the wings, which, because of the shape and incline, generates upward forces greater than the total weight of the plane."

Jake took Jessie's hand and held it outside the window of the plane. "Feel the wind on your hand, Jessie. By inclining your hand with respect to the wind, can you feel the upward or downward force?"

She nodded. "Is this what they call the 'lift-to-drag' principle?"

"Yes ... yes, that's exactly right! Aviation enthusiasts have learned that up to a certain angle where turbulence is small, lift increases. Past a certain angle, though, the smooth flow breaks down and the lift-to-drag ratio lessens rapidly. About two-thirds of the upward reaction comes from suction air pressure over the top of the curved wing and about one third from the undersurface."

Jessie asked, "How do you control the speed?"

"Air speed is a function of thrust, controlled by the engine throttle setting. This is the throttle." He pointed to a lever. "Ready to try it?"

"Oh, yeah!"

"Okay, but first, buckle up your lap and shoulder belt. With this open cockpit, might drop you out on your head!" he chuckled.

"Done. Let's go!"

Jake quickly tightened the slack on her shoulder harness, started the engine and maneuvered the plane until it had turned around in the opposite direction.

"Got to take off with the right direction in the wind," he explained.

Soon, they were airborne and Jessie felt breathless. *Ooh ... it feels so cool up here!* She watched as they climbed higher and higher and was amazed at the look of the fields, houses and terrain below. It appeared like one of Grandma's zig-zag quilts; a picture ... a miniature model of everything.

Gosh, it's incredible! She immediately understood Jake's love of flying - it felt like lightly floating ... and she did feel so free! On their turns, she watched the blazing red semi-globe of the sun slant against the horizon, exhilarated at the sense of the world tilting beneath her.

Because of the loud wind noise, Jake motioned to Jessie to watch his hand on the control instrument. She felt the movement of the plane as he moved the stick around. Jake turned to look at her and smiled as he watched her reaction - no fear whatsoever on that face; he instinctively knew she was having the same euphoric emotion he always experienced while up high like this. He began to feel a curious reaction about Jessie, one he'd not experienced with a woman before. It surprised and ... disturbed him a bit.

After a short run, only a few miles around the countryside, Jake turned the plane around and headed back to the clearing. As soon as he touched down, he heard Jessie exclaim: "Golly, *what a ride*! That was absolutely thrilling!!"

-∞-

As they rode back toward the McCarey ranch, Jake felt Jessie lean against him more heavily than on the ride out. *Poor kid, she must be exhausted.* He imagined how hard she must be working.

They reached the ranch just as the dusky sky began to concede to the dark. Jake slipped quickly off the horse and gently eased Jessie down. When Jessie asked if he'd like to come in for coffee and pie or just sit and talk awhile, Jake tenderly tilted her chin up and brushed her mouth with a soft kiss: "I think I'll pass on that nice offer tonight. Another time?"

"Sure," she smiled up at him.

Jessie watched Jake ride off, and then turned inside to find the twins and Matt waiting for her.

Snickering wickedly like a bunch of hyenas, she surmised they'd spied that kiss from behind the curtains. She sleepily turned upstairs to bed, the sweet sensation of it still caressing her lips.

Looking down over the banister she called: "Oh enjoy yourselves, you little *devils*."

| CHAPTER EIGHT |

Jake paced up and down the small hotel room. He'd been seeing Jessie McCarey now for several months and he knew without a doubt: *She was the one*. Jake had never been uptight about a woman before; of course, he'd not been anxious to marry one, either.

He'd been too busy enjoying his freedom. And, trying to drum up work. Finally, he tired of the pacing pattern around and around the room and decided to ride out to the McCarey ranch.

When Jake drew close to the house, he spied Tom and the twins reworking some sagging fences. *I'd never take for granted what that woman thinks. Maybe talking to the boys, I can get a feel for what Jessie really thinks of me.*

"Hi fellas, working hard?"

"Only when we hav-ta!" Jason joked.

"Yeah, it would be a lot easier to slack-off if'n Tom wasn't here," Josh interjected teasingly.

"Well," Jake suggested, "Why don't you three slackers take a break and talk to me about something?"

Tom looked quizzically at Jake.

| Long Horizon |

"What's up?"

"Well, I ... Well, uh ..."

"This must be about Jessie. Spit it out, man!"

Jake grinned, then grew a bit sheepish. "You're right - it is about Jessie. How do you think she feels about me?"

Tom threw his head back and laughed out loud. The twins joined in and soon they were all poking fun at Jake.

"What'd I say that's so funny? Will ya let me in on the joke?"

Tom finally regained his composure and replied: "It's just funny that you'd even have to ask, that's all."

"Well, I think she likes me and all, but I'm serious, I mean *serious* about her. I need to know, fellas."

Josh interjected: "Well, I'd say she was plum crazy 'bout ya, wouldn't you say, guys?"

Jason and Tom both nodded their agreement.

"Crazy, huh? Crazy enough to marry me, you think?"

"Marry??!!" three voices yelped all at once. "All right!!"

-∞-

When Jake reached the house, he found Kathleen and Gus McCarey snuggled together on a swing outside on the veranda. He admired, for the upteenth time, the lovely wood-framed house Gus built for his family. *Nothing like this back east*, he thought.

He tipped his hat. "Good evening, Mrs. McCarey. Sir."

"Good evening, Jacob," Kathleen answered him with one of her beautiful smiles.

"How you been, son?" Gus asked.

Jake began to relax. These people always made him feel at home - they were good people. And until lately he hadn't realized it, but he longed to be part of a real family. He'd felt an emotional distance with his father and brother for a long time.

"Oh, just fine, keeping busy drumming up work. Is Jessie around? I checked at the office in town but they said she was home today."

"Yes, she's home. Around back, Jake." Kathleen took Jake's arm and strolled toward the back of the house. She pointed, indicating where Jessie vigorously brushed up a sheen on a handsome black stallion outside the barn. Kathleen discretely turned back to continue her chat with her husband.

Jessie's sunlit hair, haphazardly pulled up with combs, moist curls escaping on her forehead and down the back of her neck, emphasized how hot and dirty she was from working on the sweaty horses. Jessie's expression showed complete surprise in Jake's visit.

Jake strolled over to a large elm tree behind the house and motioned for Jessie to follow. He could fathom the expected exasperation on her face. But before she could chew on him for coming by unexpectedly and seeing her in such a state, he leaned over and quickly silenced her with a kiss. She looked up in astonishment as he touched her face, softly wiping away a dirty smudge on her cheek with his thumb, then gently caressing a wisp of curl next to her earlobe.

"You sure look beautiful today, Miss McCarey," he said, smiling down at her.

"Well, thank you, sir. I always appreciate receiving compliments from a gentleman -- if they're genuine, that is."

"Oh, this one's genuine, all right. I think you look so gorgeous, I think ... I think I'd like to take you right into town and marry you. What would you say to that, Miss McCarey?"

He waited. Jessie stared at him for a long time. Finally: "You come out here to ask me to marry you, looking like *this?!!* I could just *kill* you, Jake Trenton!!"

"Will you marry me, first, Jessie? I need you and I don't want to be without you anymore. I'm sick of that room in town and being alone, and waking up without you and ...."

"Okay."

"What'd you say?"

"I said yes, I'll marry you. When do you want to do it? How about half an hour? I have a few more chores to do around the house, by then I'll be really good and dirty; we could do it right after the chores," she teased.

"Jessie McCarey, I love you, you wild woman."

"You better, Jake, because I ... love you, too."

"Well, that's what your brothers say!" Jake laughed.

-∞-

When Jessie explained to Jake that it would take a little while to plan the wedding, he replied that he hoped it wouldn't take <u>too</u> long. When she promised that she and Mama could probably get things arranged in a few weeks, Jake was pleased.

Each went on with their daily work routines, Jake stopping by the ranch to see her on the evenings he returned to Big Spring from his delivery routes.

Jake warned Jessie on more than one occasion about his 'wanderlust'. "I'm infected with travel, Jessie; you sure you can live with a man who roams the earth? And sky?"

"I get pretty distracted myself, Jake and sometimes tune people out. You'll have a few of *my* bad habits to get used to!"

-∞-

One rare relaxed afternoon, Jessie and MaryBeth examined fabric at Jeremiah's store in Big Spring. Jessie fussed a bit, unable to decide what material would be right for her wedding dress. She looked through various muslins and a few silks, examining each swatch by holding it in front of her face at the long, oval mirror in the corner of the store.

Jessie picked up a different bolt and asked: "Ooh! MaryBeth! What do you think of *this* color?" She put a swath of shiny, apricot-colored silk next to her face.

MaryBeth nodded approvingly. "If you're not going to wear the traditional white, that would look lovely on you; it accents your hair color."

"Well, I think I should have my own traditions. It is *my* wedding.

Of course, there is Granny Mary's dress ... For tradition's sake, Mother probably would like me to try and salvage it. Perhaps I could adjust it a bit more to my taste. Really, it's only those tight sleeves with the silly puffs I'm not fond of. What would you think if I replaced the sleeves with shorter ones, perhaps of this lacy ivory material ...?"

When MaryBeth nodded, suddenly Jessie asked, "When are you and Ben going to do this, MaryBeth?"

Caught off guard, MaryBeth blushed. "He's asked me," she shyly and quickly dropped her eyes.

Jessie laughed. "So, when are you going to agree to marry him?"

"When I get enough courage to be a married woman, I guess."

"What are you talking about? Ben adores you!"

"Well, you know, the.., the..."

"The ... what?"

MaryBeth motioned for Jessie to follow her outside. They walked behind the store and sat down on an old bench.

"Well?" Jessie questioned.

MaryBeth leaned close and whispered: "The ... married part. I don't know anything about it."

"What's there to know?"

"*Intimacy*, that's what!" Then MaryBeth looked around anxiously, to see if anyone had heard.

Jessie was taken aback. She'd never heard MaryBeth raise her voice. "Are you afraid of se.?"

"*Sh*!! *Jessie*! Somebody might hear!"

Jessie exaggeratedly whispered: "Well, that's what it is, you know." After seeing the shocked look on MaryBeth's face, she added: "Okay, 'making love,' is that better?"

"Much. Do you think it's ... difficult?"

"Difficult? Are you kidding?"

"Well, that's what Mam-maw always says. That it's something married women have to put up with. She makes it sound like men are beasts!"

Jessie threw her head back and roared with laughter. She laughed and laughed till she was nearly weak. MaryBeth waited for her to calm down and then said, "It's not funny, Jessie, I don't know what to do!"

Jessie got herself under control and put her arm around MaryBeth. "Okay, we've been friends for a long time and we've talked about a lot of things, right?"

"Yes, that's what I like about you - you'll tell me ... anything."

"You listen to me, now, and you disregard what that Grandmother of yours said, you hear me?"

"I'll try."

"At first, it may be awkward for you. I'm not going to lie to you about that. The reason I say that is because I know how embarrassed you are about undressing in front of ... even me. I've noticed it for a long time, but didn't make a fuss; afraid it might make you more timid."

"Well, I do have a little trouble with that."

"Okay, after you get undressed, Ben will want to kiss you and touch you. In places I'm sure he never has touched you ... right?"

"Oh, Ben's always been a *gentleman*!"

"Well, you need to try to relax and let him kiss you or touch you wherever he wants ..."

MaryBeth looked horrified. "Wherever?"

"Yes, wherever. I know Ben loves you and he won't be an animal, believe me. When you get used to it ... you'll love it!"

"*Jessie*!! *You <u>haven't</u>*??!!!! ... How ... do you know?"

"Oh silly goose, Mama told me. She said her great-granny had scared the be-jeebers out of women in the family about it, like your grandmother has you. But Mama believes that was probably because Great-Grampa was pretty much ... well ... a drunken louse." She giggled.

MaryBeth looked down, blushing again.

"Don't get prudish on me now. I'm telling you the truth."

"Aren't you a bit scared?"

"Sure. I guess." She grew thoughtful. "Actually, no, to be honest, I'm anxious. It's all I've thought about lately, especially when I'm spending close time with Jake. If you know what I mean ..."

MaryBeth blushed again. "Oh my goodness! I don't know if I can do this like you, Jessie."

"You can if you'll just trust yourself and trust Ben. You love him and he loves you." She grew serious. "Mama says it's the ultimate offering – the gift of yourself. And besides, you know it even says in the Bible: *the two become one.*"

"Oh, Jessie, you make it sound so wonderful! I ... well; maybe ... it will be all right!"

She noticed the look on MaryBeth's face. "Oh, quit that blushing, right now! Trust me on this; have I ever led you astray about anything?"

"Well … there was that time you got us into trouble for playing hooky and going for a dip in Miller's pond."

"Oh, other than that! You just can't let that die, can you, girl? I'll never live that one down!" Jessie chuckled and added: "I'm serious as death this time. You know I wouldn't deliberately mislead you."

When MaryBeth smiled, Jessie reached her arm around and hugged her friend again.

"We sure had some good times in school. 'Member when Roger swung way sideways on that rope at the creek and broke his arm?" Marybeth asked, giggling.

"How could I forget? Miss Riley volunteered me to write out all his homework for him. He sure enjoyed bossin' me around!"

Exchanging secret smiles, they returned to the store thinking the same thing: *It was so great to have a best friend. And now they'd be sisters.*

-∞-

A few days later, Ben approached Jessie in her office. "Have you been talking to MaryBeth?"

"She's my best friend; yes, I talk to her all the time. Why?"

"She told me today she wanted to marry me, that's what!"

"And … the problem is …?"

"I couldn't get an answer out of her till that day after you two went looking at things for your wedding. What did you say to her?"

"You mad at me?"

"Heavens, no; I'm grateful! I just wondered why she had changed so much. She seems more relaxed and happy."

"Well, I told her you loved her more than anything in this world, that you'd *die* for her, and that being married to you would be the most *wonderful* thing that ever happened in her life."

"You said all that?"

"In a manner of speaking; yes."

Ben kissed Jessie's brow. "Thanks ever so much, Sis."

"You just make sure you don't ever let her down, you hear me? I know you love her, but don't you *ever* hurt her! She's so delicate, so fragile. You might be my big brother, but I'll make you pay if you do …" Jessie made a fake, menacing scowl.

"I won't, I swear."

Ben smiled and Jessie softly answered, "I know." Then added: "How about making it a double wedding?"

"You mean it?! You wouldn't mind?"

"She's my best friend, remember?"

-∞-

Jessie and MaryBeth talked their fiancés into setting the wedding date in May. The girls wanted an outdoor ceremony and felt that by that time, the weather would cooperate. It did. The twelfth of May was a gorgeous Oklahoma day. Trees and prairie grasses painted the landscape vibrant green, brilliant wildflowers sprang up everywhere, dotting the green with perfuse colors. Unexpected but appreciated: little wind. Perfect day for a wedding.

Jessie's brothers did all the expected mean things -- wrote teasing little signs and left them everywhere, put rice in her bed the night before, poked their heads into her room several times to see if they could catch her in her underwear so she'd shriek at them. It went on all day.

MaryBeth brought her things to the McCarey home in the afternoon so they could get ready for the ceremony together. As the girls were giggling together, Kathleen gently knocked on the door. When Jessie asked her to come in, Kathleen told the girls how lovely they looked and hugged each of them.

As Kathleen was about to leave, Jessie quickly put her arms around her Mother and drew her back.

"I know I don't tell you often enough, Mama, but I love you very much. Thank you for everything you do – you're *always* here for me when I need you. Times like this make me stop to appreciate things … like you sewing the altered sleeves on my dress, playing the music, detailing the cake, flowers, all the lovely things you've arranged for this wedding."

Kathleen replied: "I've so enjoyed planning this wonderful day with MaryBeth's Mother. It's been such fun; we've become even closer friends. And, it's the least I could do for my girls – now I'll have *two* daughters!"

Kathleen kissed Jessie's cheek, then turned and kissed MaryBeth.

As she quickly wiped away a happy tear: "I better get downstairs to set up the piano arrangement while the two of you finish dressing."

As Kathleen softly closed the door behind her, MaryBeth picked up some minuscule apricot-colored flowers lying on the dresser.

"I asked Matthew earlier if he could pick some wildflowers in the meadow down by the creek. I told him the colors I wanted and he's such a sweetheart -- was so excited, he flew off to help. See what Matty found … they are just perfect; so delicate."

"Wow, you remembered that's my favorite color!"

MaryBeth brushed Jessie's long hair till it glowed, and then gently French-twisted the silky sides, plaiting a few loose braids in the long curls in back, and then entwining tiny bits of the flowers into those braids.

Jessie helped MaryBeth adjust her veil, and stood back, awestruck at MaryBeth.

"You're *exquisite!* With those golden curls and sky-blue eyes, you're like a fragile, porcelain doll. No … an angel!"

"*You're* the one that's beautiful," MaryBeth replied. She smiled adoringly at Jessie, who'd decided against wearing a veil. "Your hair looks like Gwenevere's. You've such vibrant beauty; you don't even need decoration, Jessie."

"Well, we'd best get down to the two luckiest men in Oklahoma, before they change their minds," Jessie teased.

-∞-

The McCarey and Stockton families and many friends gathered outside. The men had set up rows of chairs and tables along the side, to hold the huge cakes, china and arrangements of flowers Kathleen and MaryBeth's mother had lovingly created. Jason and Josh acted as ushers, flirting outrageously, all the while escorting the ladies to their seats.

As the girls came down the back stairs, Gus took Jessie's arm and MaryBeth's father grasped hers. Gus pecked Jessie's cheek, as he escorted her around the corner to the back porch. There he nodded for Kathleen to start playing the piano.

The lively chatter quieted. Gus and Jessie walked down the aisle created by space between the rows of chairs, Mr. Stockton following with MaryBeth.

As they turned to watch the lovely sight coming toward them, Ben extended a handshake to Jake. When they reached the grooms standing under a trellis of flowers, Gus placed Jessie's hand in Jake's and Mr. Stockton tenderly kissed and laid MaryBeth's hand into Ben's.

Pastor Murphy beamed as ladies sniffed into their hankies. After a moment, he began:

"I have known the McCarey and Stockton families for a long time now. Ben, Jessica and MaryBeth have been like my own children – I've come to love each of them for their rare qualities. And it's been a real pleasure getting to know Jake these past weeks -- I already sense he is a fine man. Miss Jessie, here, is *lucky* to have him."

The pastor winked at Jake. As the audience chuckled, Jessie wrinkled up her nose, and then grinned at the minister.

"Jake, before you're committed, you do understand Jessie is quite the wild one, don't you?"

Everyone roared this time, MaryBeth fighting to suppress her giggle. Ben bit his lip. And Jake winked at the minister.

"It is always a pleasure to assist wonderful young people such as these engage in that practice God so highly esteems: the holy state of marriage. It is not something to be entered into lightly, but reverently. So now, I must become serious." He paused.

"These two couples come before us today, of their own free will, to join in this glorious state. If there be any present who have reason why they should not be joined together, let him state so now, or forever hold his peace."

After a short period of silence: "Then, let us begin. Would you bow with me?" The two couples knelt before the pastor.

"Lord, please bless these fine young people. Give them Your love; send them the Spirit of Your Presence, to help them throughout all the days of their lives. We thank you for your blessings and ask this in the name of your beloved Son, Jesus."

The congregation joined in: "*Amen.*"

Pastor Murphy indicated the couples should rise. Then: "Do you, MaryBeth, take Benjamin, to have and to hold, to love and to cherish, in sickness and in heath, until death do you part?"

"Yes, I will."

"Do you, Benjamin, take MaryBeth, to love and cherish, for better, for worse, in sickness and in health, til death do you part?"

"Yes, Sir, I do."

"And, do you, Sarah Jessica, take Jacob ..."

"Yes."

The minister looked intently at Jessie. "I hadn't finished your part, Sarah, I wonder if I need to put in the 'obey' clause?"

"If you really think it's necessary ...?" She smiled innocently.

"Let's just continue ... do you, Jacob, take Jessica, to love and to cherish, for better, for worse, in sickness and in health, til death do you part?"

"I most certainly do."

The minister indicated to the best men, (Tom and MaryBeth's brother, Harry) that they should extend the rings. After Ben slipped MaryBeth's gently on her finger and Jake placed Jessie's on hers:

"I now pronounce that these two couples are ... uh ... men and wives. That seems a bit awkward. How about ... man and wife ... and man and wife?"

As the audience chuckled, Jake looked tenderly down at Jessie and whispered: "I promise I'll always love you, Jessie McCarey - Trenton, don't you ever forget that!"

"You'd *better*, Mister!"

Jake smiled and watched Ben give MaryBeth a gentle kiss, as the audience clapped for them. But Jake roughly brought Jessie into his arms and gave her a rousing kiss that lasted a *long* few minutes. Everyone clapped again, whispered deliciously and then heartily laughed before it ceased.

| CHAPTER NINE |

The next few months passed quickly. Big Spring grew as Oklahoma's population continued to boom. A second surge of oil discoveries between 1915 and 1920 established nearby Tulsa as the "Oil Capital of the World," where oilmen such as William Skelly and J. Paul Getty built stately mansions and modern headquarters.

Big Spring was not as large, but per capita, its income rivaled many of the larger cities. As McCarey Oil's exploration also boomed, work became frantic for Jessie. It seemed she spent scant time at home. And when she *was* at the tiny apartment she and Jake rented in town, she stayed busy sprucing it a bit - cleaning, painting, building shelves to expand the limited space.

Jake didn't seem to mind, though, because building his delivery routes filled his time. Jessie tried to keep his route schedule on her desk, but due to the nature of his cargo, plans changed so frequently she found it difficult to keep her copy up to date. His runs varied from Big Spring to Kansas City to St. Louis, or Tulsa to Wichita. He occasionally had a longer run to New Orleans, also. Jake's schedule made it hectic for him, but as long as he appeared happy, Jessie was content.

Business was so good for the family Jessie bought a car to drive back and forth from work, home and out to the drilling sites. Even though busy juggling projects at the office, she occasionally made time to see how the field operations were going. She relished getting outdoors, never tiring of the scenery down the country roads.

On one trip in the car they'd purchased, filled with supplies, she weaved through the rough, nearly un-navigable paths, crossing low streams and passing wagons pulled by horses. Many of the 'roads' were nothing more than old Indian trails. She gingerly eased her car behind a wagon, being careful not to get stuck on the higher part of the ruts. *Should-a driven the boys' truck!*

Jessie determined to bring the board of directors out here for a visit. *See the way the money's made; let them get their hands a little dirty.* Her instinct told her that might really get them fired up for the new projects she had in mind. Watching the hands 'spud in' (begin drilling) or 'making a trip' (changing out drilling parts) was much more exciting than reading a description in a progress report.

Jessie's full attention lately concentrated on convincing the board that they should enter into a joint venture with the Townsends' company, to build a railroad spur from their producing fields to the main S&O rail line. A new concept, one the board was skeptical of, particularly because Townsend Oil was one of their main competitors. But she had Ben all prepped for battle with figures for the board. She'd done her homework and felt this spur would be crucial to them, if oil prices ever went up.

However, with the glut of crude oil on the market (crude price had dropped from a dollar and five cents to thirty-five cents a barrel) and the economic condition of the whole country, it would be difficult to sell the board on this proposal. But that was exactly the reason for the co-venture: to raise the needed capital.

Jessie always looked toward the future; she knew that if this company were to survive, they would have to be aggressive in their decision-making. Lately, she and Ben were exasperated at the board's lack of confidence in their proposals. *Why, look at what hiring those chemists and setting up a Research and Development group in the company had done-- they were selling products that had previously been burned off or dumped as waste material!* Their gasoline production increased and she felt confident that the market would soon take off, as more and more automobiles were sold.

They'd located a plant to extract the liquids from the natural gas, with a method of cooling and condensing the gas vapors. The innovative ideas and resulting patents their chemists were pulling off was impressive. *The catalytic research alone looked promising …*

When she reached their latest drilling site, Jessie visited with Tom for awhile about the operation's beginnings. "Tommie, remember when we first started? How much trouble the men gave me?"

"You kiddin'? How could I forget?"

"Well, I heard on the news last night that several women who picketed the White House for voting rights some weeks ago were severely beaten and jailed."

"Yeah, it's a wonder anyone ever found out where they were; some were nearly dead before their families discovered they'd been jailed and got them released."

"If even our own President believes women who want rights should be institutionalized, I am one lucky woman."

"I hope they'll be all right. Sad, really. No one deserves that kind of treatment."

"They are so brave. Think we'll ever get to vote?"

Tom shrugged his shoulders: "Dunno - beats me."

"Well, I want you to know how much I appreciate your support. I'm so blessed to have such protective brothers. It can't be easy, constantly defending your crazy sister."

"It's my honor, Jess. You proved your mettle -- you've got a good head for business. By the way, want to run something by ya: you know, over on the Townsend leases they keep building new rigs, but I think we should come up with somethin' we can move from site to site."

"Oh, you're getting *into* this business thing, now?" she teased.

"Yeah, guess so; you've even convinced me, an old hardhead. You always get your way, don't ya, Jess?"

"Not always, but extremely pleased I did this time. So glad we've been able to put our differences aside and work together. It's meant more to me than I can tell you, brother," she added softly.

"Me too, Jess."

"By the way, that's a *fan-*tastic idea: 'portable rigs' – now who would have thought of that but you, Tommie?" Jessie asked proudly.

| CHAPTER TEN |
1916

Something frightening Jessie lately: all the activity in Europe. With Germany at war with its neighboring countries, rumor was that the U.S. might soon be involved. She worried about the men in her family: would they be required to enter the service? Jake had even mentioned that a representative from the Army Air Corps contacted him about possibly training new recruits. She knew Jake: if asked to help out, he would. And she was still a tad put-out at him for those crazy *loop-de-loops* and that terrifying downward plunge, showing off at the fair last month.

As if that wasn't enough, things had been so hectic lately with the company. That blasted fire at their new refinery last week! [She shuddered.] Jessie was so relieved Tom was on-site; he always knew the best action to take in an emergency. Though a few employees had minor burns, everyone felt fortunate there were no fatalities. They had to face a hard fact: the refining business was dangerous.

Ben visited all the injured employees to determine the cause, so they could try to prevent future accidents. And when he reassured them about their jobs – the employees were gratefully mindful that this was a family-operated company.

To get her mind off her worries, Jessie dreamed of Christmas - her favorite holiday. She began selecting gifts for the family: a gorgeous red velvet dress for her mother, some of that aromatic pipe tobacco her father liked so well that Jake found in South Carolina, sweaters and shirts for her brothers. She debated and debated about what to get Jake - maybe one of those sharp leather jackets she'd seen advertised in the catalog. She wanted their first Christmas together to be special and remained continually thankful they were all doing so well financially.

Jessie grew thoughtful. Thinking about her family holidays together led to wondering what Jake's family was like. She assumed they were well-off, though he didn't talk much about them. Most of what she'd been able to get out of him was that when his mother died several years ago, his father immersed himself into his publishing firm. Because Jake had no interest in the business, he grew alienated from his father. Jake told Jessie he felt guilty that they had grown so far apart, even angry with each other at times, but his guilt became tempered somewhat by the fact that his brother, William, had gone into the business with his father.

Jessie sensed Jake must be unhappy without his family. He fit in so well with hers; she knew he was happy here, but thought that he must surely miss his own. She suddenly determined to do something about it! She searched through Jake's records and found his father's address. Taking quite some time composing her thoughts, Jessie wrote Mr. Trenton a letter. She spontaneously invited him for Christmas dinner with her family, saying she would really enjoy getting to know him.

She tried not to get her hopes up, but thought a great deal about it over the next few weeks.

As the days grew closer to the holidays, Jake became somewhat reclusive and mysterious. Jessie wondered if he was getting depressed or just working too hard.

Early Christmas morning when Jessie woke, she softly kissed her sleeping husband and sashayed to the kitchen to brew their coffee. Enjoying a steaming cup in the tiny kitchenette of their apartment, she gazed outside, enchanted at the light snowfall outside, painting the windowpane with frosty lace. This was unusual in Oklahoma – it snowed occasionally, but bestowed a rare treat for Christmas day. While she dreamily watched the flakes dance, Jake quietly sneaked up behind her and grabbed her around the neck, affectionately biting her ear.

"Jake! What are you doing?"

"Kissing Mrs. Trenton, that's what. You got any complaints?"

"No, sir, just don't stop there," she giggled.

"Where's my present, woman!? Didn't you get me anything for Christmas?" he mocked.

"Of course I did - can't you see all that stuff under the tree?"

Jake went into the living area, and crawling around on the floor, scrambled all through the packages, looking for any with his name on it. There were none. "What's this?" he said, of a big decorated box he'd found minus a name.

"Well, I guess that must be yours," she teased. "And maybe that one, too." She pointed beneath the larger one.

He tore the wrapping off the first package and opened the box. Inside he found the leather jacket Jessie had ordered for him from the catalog, and matching boots.

"Just like the fliers wear. But you're gonna look so good in them, I better not catch any women in that plane!" she teased.

Slumping down next to him, she held out the other package. Inside Jake found a thin, flat bronzed plaque, embossed: *Ace Trenton.*

"It's to be mounted on the front of your plane," she explained.

"Oh, baby, this is so great; thanks! Now for your presents." He walked to the desk and pulled out a small package.

Jessie untied a velvet bow and found inside a heart-shaped gold locket and chain. "Jake, it's exquisite!"

"Look inside - there's more."

She gently pulled the sides apart and inside lay a tiny piece of paper, folded. She stretched it out and read: *Get in the car, we're going for a ride to find the rest of your Christmas present.*

"What's this, Jake?"

"Get dressed and I'll show you."

"We'll have to hurry. I promised to come early and help Mama cook dinner."

"Won't take long. It's right on the way toward your folks' place."

-∞-

They drove about a mile from town and Jake hopped out of the car, running to her side. He held out his hand for Jessie. "Look all around you, Mrs. Trenton. What do you think of this place?"

The snow had ceased and the sun came out. She twirled around, where sunlight glistening on ice and melting snow left a blanket of a million sparkling diamonds, turning the landscape brilliant.

"Well, it's a beautiful spot, Jake, but what's this all about?"

"I've bought this acreage for you. I want to build a house for us here, as soon as I can afford it."

"Jake!! Are you kidding?! This is ours?"

"Yes, Ma'am. Well... it *will* be after I make the next eighteen payments, but it'll go fast. When I can get the financing for the house, we'll start building."

"I think I might be able to get the money."

"No, *I* want to do this, for you, for us, Jess. Let me see how I can do it, okay?"

Jessie gazed around at the area – lots of nice, established trees and a large pond out back. She put her hands in front of her in the air, as if framing it for a photograph.

"I want a big window on this side. A big living room and a gigantic fireplace – you know, a masculine, rustic look, like a lodge. And the kitchen over there -- though I don't know when I'll have time to cook for you."

He smiled as he watched her making mental notes. "We'll hire a cook. What do you think?" he asked excitedly.

"It's amazing! She planted on him a passionate kiss.

Then: "Let's go tell the family!"

-∞-

Excited, they drove to Jessie's parents' house at the ranch and she immediately went to the kitchen to see her Mother. MaryBeth had already arrived, and the ladies worked together, preparing the meal while they chattered excitedly about Jessie's news.

After all were assembled at the table, MaryBeth glanced at Ben and asked softly: "okay … now?"

When Ben nodded affirmatively, MaryBeth shyly announced: "Ben and I also have some good news to share. We're expecting a baby in June!"

Everyone was ecstatic; pandemonium broke out around the table.

Jason started yelling: "I'm gonna be an uncle, an uncle!"

"Me, too!" Josh added.

"And me … I'm old enough, ain't I?" Matthew chorused.

MaryBeth smiled and hugged Matt. "You sure are, and you'll make a wonderful uncle." She looked around. "This baby is blessed to have all of you, and Grandma and Grandpa McCarey. And Auntie Jessie …"

Tom and Stephen roughly nudged Ben, teasing: "You old dog."

Gus finally put up his big hands and admonished, "We must give thanks."

Everyone quieted down, bowed their heads as he began: "Dear Lord, we know all blessings come from You. We thank You for Your bounty, and especially the gift of family. Please bless us all, especi'lly MaryBeth and Ben, and the new little one soon to grace this table. In Jesus' name …"

All: "Amen."

It one of the best Christmases Jessie could remember; so wonderful having the family all together again, especially now that she and Jake and MaryBeth and Ben lived away from home.

-∞-

That evening, the women heated up leftovers and called the men from the kitchen to eat supper. Just as they all gathered around the big table, they heard a knock at the front door. Jason answered it, and then called into the dining room: "*someone here to see Jessie!*"

When she walked to the front door, a stranger stood there, but he seemed somewhat familiar. He smiled and asked: "Sarah, is your dinner invitation still open?"

She suddenly realized it was Jake's father, took his hand, then reached up and embraced him. He initially seemed a little startled by her quick gesture, but relaxed and smiled at her.

"Come in and meet my family," she said as she led him to the dining room.

Near the end of the table, Jake joked and laughed with Josh and Jason, good-naturedly teasing them about some of the girls in town. He looked up as Jessie and his father entered the room, completely shaken to see him.

"Hello, Son, how are you?" Jake's father asked.

"I'm fine, Sir. How? ... When?"

"I just arrived today and found a fellow that offered to drive me here. People certainly are accommodating in this part of the country."

"This is unexpected!" Jake ejected. Then he strode toward his father and awkwardly extended his hand.

"Well, Darling," Jessie sheepishly explained, "I wrote your father a letter a few weeks back and when I didn't hear anything from him ... I didn't mention it, Jake. I didn't want you to be disappointed if he couldn't come."

"Oh, I'm forgetting my manners! Mr. Trenton, I'd like to introduce you to my family … this is my mother, Kathleen; my father, Gus. This is my dear sister-in-law, MaryBeth; over there are my brothers: Tom, Jason, Ben, Stephen, Josh and that's Matt."

"It's a pleasure to meet all of you," Mr. Trenton replied.

"We've leftovers from dinner, but glad to have you here for Christmas supper, Mr. Trenton. Please sit down and make yourself at home," Kathleen graciously offered. "What a wonderful surprise for Jake!"

"Thank you very much, Mrs. McCarey. And please call me Andrew."

"Well, Andrew, we're surely glad to have ya with us," said Gus, as he mightily pumped Mr. Trenton's hand. "Sit down, please. Matt, run into the kitchen and get another plate for Andrew?"

"Yes, sir! I'll be right back!"

Andrew Trenton scrutinized his son's expression across the table. Still that awkward reserve between them. *Maybe I made a mistake coming here.* Then he watched as Jessie sat down next to Jake and gently caressed his cheek with her hand. Jake smiled and put his arm around her - *that look on his face is close to adoration*, Andrew thought. Reminded him of how he had felt about Jake's mother. Andrew took an immediate liking to Jessie - something that surprised him as it usually took a while to size someone up. He began to relax.

"Mr. Trenton, Jake and I just told the family today that we're buying some land close to Big Spring and planning to build a home there. How long will you be here? We'd love to take you out to see it."

"Oh, I'll be here a few days. I figured if I came all this way, I might as well see a little of this wild country I've always heard about back East."

"Well, you'll have to stay with us, at our apartment," Jessie exclaimed. "We can put you up on our chaise lounger …"

"Oh, I couldn't impose. I've taken a room at the hotel in town."

"That place is a rat-trap!" exclaimed Kathleen. "We've got room here, Andrew, and you are more than welcome to stay with us."

"I couldn't take advantage of your hospitality. The offer of such a delicious-smelling meal is more than generous."

"It's no problem a'tall," Gus soothed. "No problem a'tall. Jason, after supper's over, you take Mr. Trenton into town in that crazy contraption of a car and pick up his things. Then you bring him right back out here." Looking resolutely at Andrew: "And we won't take *no* for an answer!"

Andrew Trenton quickly understood why Jake had settled in Oklahoma. It was obvious that Jake had bonded as a real part of this warm, boisterous family. It saddened him that their relationship wasn't as comfortable, but hoped that he and Jake would have a chance to patch things up between them before he left.

Soon, dishes were passed to Andrew from all sides and he enjoyed the pleasure of joyous chatter and a scrumptious meal.

"Don't forget to save room for some of my chocolate-pecan pie," Marybeth added. Bestowing upon him one of her sweet smiles, Andrew Trenton was entirely smitten.

-∞-

The next day, as Jessie and Jake 'toured' Mr. Trenton around the countryside, Jessie gave him a history lesson about the area. Andrew seemed captivated by her enthusiastic descriptions.

Jake silently drove while Jessie chattered on, relishing her father-in-law's company. After one particularly spirited story, Andrew asked: "You really love this country, don't you, Sarah?"

"Yes, Sir, I do. It's such a young state, but the exciting (and complicated) history of Oklahoma goes back much farther. This frontier community was created by people who had dreams of a new beginning. To truly understand how people come to love it so much, you have to picture what struggles they went through. I've had an easy, happy life, but for the settlers, like my Mama and Papa, it was tough."

"I can only imagine."

"In the early years people lived in tents, sod huts or makeshift houses built of anything they could get their hands on. They worked from sun-up til sun-down, with ceaseless worry about crops, weather, money, and most of all, about their children, who died at an alarming rate. More than half of all the settlers had children die at birth or in the early years. Our family is an exception – we've been very fortunate."

"The desolation and isolation in the remote areas must have been very hard, especially for the women," Andrew said.

"Yes, Sir, that's truly insightful. But Oklahomans in the rural areas visit back and forth regularly with their neighbors. Usually it's helping someone build their home. Get-togethers are busy affairs, with little drinking or carousing, and all make a great effort to be happy. Despite the competitiveness of the various land runs, the Oklahoma countryside is generally a neighborly place where people are united by common challenges."

"Isn't it dangerous in places?"

"In the 'oil boom' towns, you have a lot of turmoil and some crime, but not in the farming areas and outlying settlements."

Andrew voiced his agreement: "It seems like a very peaceful community out here."

"You know our family is Irish? I'm especially proud of the Irish contribution to Oklahoma history."

"I assumed that, yes," Andrew answered. "Where is your family originally from?"

"Well, originally Shannon, but my father hails from Virginia, and he met my mother in Georgia."

"How did he convince her to come here to this wild West? That must have been quite a convincing argument," he laughed.

"Yes, it was, especially considering that Mama came from a fairly well-off family and her father had a complete fit about her marrying my poor Papa. But she was so crazy in love with him she went against her father's wishes. It was terribly hard for her: I know how much she loved …I should say, worshipped, her father, but Papa is the only man for her. We've never heard from her family so I think Mama's father disinherited her."

"That must be hard," Andrew said quietly.

"Yes, but someday I hope to get to Georgia and I'm going to go right up to that stubborn old man and tell him I'm his granddaughter! That's a kick in his pants he's had coming a long time … don't you think?"

She laughed and Andrew joined in. This was certainly one of the most spirited women he'd ever encountered. He glanced over at his son, who continued smiling with patronizing nods; as if he were smart enough not to get involved when Jessie was like this. Jake knew once she got started on family history, she could go on for some time, but it amused him nonetheless.

"Jessie," Jake started, "Father may want to see some other places today, but I really need to make a quick run to Tulsa this afternoon. Would you mind driving me to the airfield and entertaining him until I get back this evening?"

"No, darling, I'd *enjoy* the time with your Father."

She turned to Andrew: "This will give you a chance to see Jake's plane. It's much warmer today than yesterday – typical Oklahoma weather! It can be below zero one day, and almost light-jacket comfortable the next. After dropping Jake off, you and I will head out to a gorgeous spot overlooking the prairie where our home will be, for a picnic lunch. I brought a blanket to spread out, but if it's too cool, we'll just eat in the automobile. We'll still have a gorgeous view of the valley and prairie below."

"That sounds like a real treat."

-∞-

Later, after eating delicious fried chicken and apple pie from the large basket Jessie prepared, she and Andrew sat on an old patch quilt, leaning back against a tree with another quilt covering them up, gazing out over the wide expanse of tall-grass prairie. At a distance, bison grazed.

"See those tall trees? That's the acreage Jake bought to build our house. In the meantime, I escape out here. Jake loves travel and being up alone in his plane, but this is where I retreat. I've always loved this area. I know it's selfish, since *we've* used up parts of it, but I hope not all of the open country will be settled. That it stays beautiful, unspoiled and wild like this."

Andrew dreamily stared at the wide sweep of blue horizon before him, so dramatically contrasting with the golden sea of dried grass and brownish leaves remaining. No trace remained of the light snowfall from two days earlier. The sun so bright; it seemed almost spring-like.

After awhile, Andrew asked: "Tell me more, Jessie. You were talking about the Irish settlers when Jake mentioned he needed to leave."

"I hope I'm not boring you with all that."

"Absolutely not. You're not boring me at all. I think it's all quite fascinating! Please continue."

"I'm so glad to hear you ask, because I love our history. Let's see, the Irish … our family has been successful, with ranching, but certainly not famous. But, there are a lot of Irish people who've made great contributions to Oklahoma history. Even women! Though I'm not related to them, makes me proud."

"Tell on …"

"One was a grandmotherly woman from County, Cork, Ireland called 'Mother Jones,' who led strikes, went to jail frequently, and won the respect of the nation's miners. Mining is an important business here, you know. In 1906, she *packed* United Worker union halls throughout what was then Indian Territory with her rousing tirades."

"Mother Jones, eh? Sounds like a remarkable woman."

"She must have been a corker! Wish I'd known her. Another was Kate Barnard, an active reformer in the cause of children's rights, prison reform and women's suffrage."

"Did she encounter a lot of problems? I imagine strong women were a bit … um … held back?"

"Perhaps, but still she helped build an Oklahoma prison where prisoners were treated humanely, and recovered *two million dollars* budgeted for use by Indian orphans that some crooked politicians misappropriated."

Jessie added somewhat sheepishly: "All of Oklahoma history isn't pretty – we've had some pretty wild political activity here. And not all of it above-board. Probably the best known Irish*man* in Oklahoma would be Dennis Flynn. Because of his political talent, he was nominated as a delegate from what was then the Territory."

"I suppose that was before Oklahoma became a State?"

"Yes, delegates had no vote in Congress at that time. He was instrumental in drumming up interest for the gradual annexation of Indian Territory into Statehood. He worked hard on behalf of homesteaders and was considered the most effective campaigner to appear in Oklahoma politics."

When Andrew nodded for her to continue, Jessie winked.

Andrew chuckled: "Sounds like a lively story coming …"

"You'll find this amusing: In 1901, an Irishman named Frank Murray was arrested by tribal police for something … about having eight white tenants on his farm in violation of Chickasaw law. Rather than pay his high-priced lawyer, (who, by the way, later became an Oklahoma governor) he bought a jug of whiskey for the jury, which they *consumed*."

"Did it help his case?"

"Yep, was acquitted. Isn't that just outrageous?? But typical of the spirit of the early settlers," she laughed.

"What about the Indian history?"

"Oh, it would take eons to tell you about that! We'd like to drive you to Pawhuska tomorrow where the leases are purchased at the Indian Agency. I don't know whether they'll be having tribal dances; hopefully some before you leave. It is wonderful to experience."

She sighed. "I wish it were summer. There's an infamous barbeque, "The Outlaws and Cow Thieves Reunion," at a local ranch owned by a generous, fellow oilman. Law officials as well as wanted criminals mingle freely. The outlaws have amnesty during that get-together, so it's an opportunity for some to wheedle for a reduced sentencing deal and turn themselves in. If not, they are free to walk away, unmolested by the deputies. However, all bets are *off* by the next morning," she laughed.

"My! That sounds truly adventurous! I'd enjoy attending that unique event!" Andrew exclaimed, raising his eyebrows.

"Many diverse people, and particularly the Indians, certainly made their contributions to the colorful past of this place. I doubt people know of the hardships they endured and that many weren't savages, but educated, cultured people – particularly those called *The Five Civilized Tribes*."

"I've heard that expression, but frankly, don't know which tribes it refers to."

"Cherokee, Creek, Choctaw, Chickasaw and Seminole. Did you know the Cherokee had their own written language?"

"Seems I heard something about it."

"Many people don't understand a particularly tragic part of Oklahoma history, and U.S. history: those native people were forcibly separated from their families in the East. Removed from their homes and driven here. Many died on the journey; one such movement known as 'The Trail of Tears.' Few know what the process of moving the Indians did to their spirit. The more fortunate were the hunters, for those tribes had no oil money and their allotments aren't sufficient for as much exploitation by the whites."

"You've a great deal of respect for the Indians, don't you Sarah?"

"Yes, I've generally found them to be loving parents to their children and they have such reverent respect for this land. Some tribes were successful starting over, only to be punished again after the Civil War for Oklahoma's general sympathy for the South. Of course, even a few Indians held slaves here before the war, so that had to be dealt with."

She hesitated. "I'm sorry; I've rattled on quite a while …"

"You've really enlightened me on facts I had no knowledge of, Sarah. It's been a fascinating historical journey for me."

"This is a fascinating place, Mr. Trenton; a true frontier. It's hard to articulate, really, but I cherish the spirit of the people here. You'll find Oklahomans to be spontaneous and warm, with a deep reverence for the beauty of the land. There is something mystical about these rocks and hills that make them special. I can't put my finger on it … it's …"

"Perhaps you mean: '*Je ne sais quo*', as the French would say. I think I understand, Sarah. Oklahoma seems like a state of many countries. Thank you for a most delightful afternoon."

"My pleasure."

-∞-

Four days later, as Jessie and Jake bade Andrew goodbye at the train station, Jessie wiped a tear from her eye and hugged her father-in-law for a long time. Andrew and Jake still had things to make up for, but the bitterness and tension between them was much better. Andrew was happy he'd made the trip to Oklahoma and was doubly glad that Jake had married such a level-headed woman.

"Goodbye, children, I must say I really enjoyed this visit. Sarah, that barbequed buffalo we had the other day was an unexpected treat! Thank you for your invitation, my dear."

"I'm just so glad you could come! Please visit us again and I'm going to try to get Jake to bring me East. Then you can be *my* tourist guide and show and tell me all about *your* beautiful city." She added softly: "I'll write you from time to time, if you'd like."

"I'd like that very much. And … if you'd call me … 'Dad'?"

He briefly touched his arm around Jake's shoulders, gave Jessie a kiss on her cheek and walked to the train steps. They watched until Andrew climbed into the car door and turned. He waved a last time before disappearing inside.

"Jessie, you are some kind of woman," Jake said, as he waved goodbye to his father.

"Oh really? How so?"

"I never thought I'd see the day Andrew Trenton would come to Oklahoma. But he acted like he actually enjoyed himself. Think you've got him wrapped around your little finger."

"I don't know about that. My family helped, you know."

"Yes, you're probably right about that. Maybe he saw what a real family should be. Earlier, I might have been mad at you for inviting him without telling me, but seeing how it affected the old man, I have to say that I'm grateful."

"Well, I'm glad it worked out. And *you* can help me write those letters to him I promised ..."

-∞-

Jessie's joy over the success of her father-in-law's visit was overshadowed by more news of the war going in Europe. The latest insinuated that the U.S. might be caught up in it before long.

The newspapers related that the first American troops arrived in France in June 1917, approximately 200,000 Yankees in training. They encountered fierce warfare and Americans began learning about poison gas, hand grenades and demolition.

She mentally cursed the Germans and their power-hungry ideas. *Why should they invade her private, wonderful world?* The only good thing about it was after the lull in the price of crude oil, prices began to rocket. They were all making a lot of money.

| CHAPTER ELEVEN |
December, 1917

Josh stopped by the family office to say a last goodbye to Jessie and Ben. His army unit was leaving for England, and then on to Europe for combat duty. Jessie had been optimistic that Josh wouldn't be sent overseas. But now she had to face reality.

Ben extended his hand to their brother, and quickly embraced him. But Jessie held and hugged Josh, afraid to let him go. Josh might be the only member of the family involved in the war, but Jessie felt even one was too much to risk. She knew that was selfish and determined to be brave, blinked back tears and put on a smile for Josh as she kissed him goodbye.

"Need a ride to the station?" Ben offered.

"No, Jason's outside, he'll see me off from there." He gazed at Jessie. "Will you write me, Sis?"

"You bet! Don't ever forget -- we love you, brother."

Jessie watched as he walked out the office; then she ran to the window, waving and gazing longingly after him until he and Jason drove out of sight.

Jake had, as anticipated, been asked to help indoctrinate some of the new recruits in the basics of flying, but as the military was not yet using planes, training was limited. Jessie was guiltily relieved that Jake wasn't called for active duty.

Before the war started, crude dropped from $1.05 to thirty-five cents a barrel. Now the war speculations drove the price back up to $3.50 a barrel. But the family was saddened that they should profit from others' misfortune. Ben and Jessie labored with government contractors, to help ensure fuel supplies stayed continuous. The family's business was profitable; it only felt right to do their part. They fervently hoped their efforts would help bring Josh safely home.

The McCarey family listened intently to the radio for news from overseas. Whenever Jessie could get away from the office early, she drove out to the ranch and joined the nightly family vigil. It kept the family close, in their united hope for Josh's safety.

Jessie eagerly awaited Josh's rare letters from France. At first, they were chatty, talking about all the grunts in his outfit, the mischief they got into, etc. In one, he spoke of a girl named Michelle that he met outside a rural village. He said she was very pretty and a nice friend.

Jessie laughed at one particularly-descriptive narration of Josh and Michelle 'making out' (kissing) as they rode down the winding French roads on <u>separate</u> bicycles. It comforted Jessie, knowing Josh had such a sweet friend. But in March she received a letter that clutched at her heart:

Dear Jessie:

Everthing is quiet here for now, so thot I'd write some letters. Hope you are well. Our outfit moved here to DuMond, a small town near Paris yesterday. There has been some fighting here close by, the other unit told us, but we haven't seen action yet here.

Last week in Bordeaux, (hope this is spelled right, I saw it on a road sign, sounds like Bordo) we were attacked at night by German fire. It was really scarey, but you know, once I grabbed my rifle and started firin back, was too busy to worry. It is the strangest feeling, really, I know I should be a good solger, but I hope I didn't kill anyone.

I'll be happy when this is over so I can come home. Some of the other boys are real nervous, specially on night watch, cause you can't see nothin. I try to keep their spirits up and have some good friends. We all watch each others back. I just keeping thinking about Michelle and you all back home and that keeps me going.

Jess, hope you don't mind me writing this kind of stuff, but I just need to talk to someone. It helps to get it out. And I only write Mama like, it's pretty here, the French people are nice, and so on. Don't tell her I'm scared, OK? It will only worrie her.

I think about you and remember all our fun and pranks together. And all the help you gave me with my schoolwork. You are a good sister and I miss you lots. Write back!

Love <u>always</u>,
Your brother Josh

The radio broadcasts didn't supply all the ghastly details of the war. But what the news didn't furnish, the McCarey siblings visualized from

Josh's hints about the real details: artillery coupled with machine guns made crossing open ground extremely dangerous. The Germans introduced poison gas, soon used by both sides. Its effects were brutal, causing slow and painful death. Commanders failed to develop tactics for breaching entrenched positions without heavy casualties. When the family speculated about some of these details, they ensured it wasn't in the presence of Kathleen...

Jessie did write back – she mailed Josh at least two letters a week, keeping him updated on the business, their family, people and events in Big Spring he would be interested in. Trying her best to keep his morale up, she contrived lively, over-the-top hilarious, (sometimes a bit decadent) letters about the crazy local people they knew.

And she did a lot of praying.

1918

In May, the McCareys were encouraged by an Allied victory. Finally, the news reported that in the tiny French village of Cantigny, Americans, in their first offensive of the war, took the town in less than an hour, aiding their British and French counterparts! Everyone believed the war would soon be over. And Josh would come home.

-∞-

On August 16, an official telegram arrived at the McCarey home from the United States Army. It bore crushing, sad news that *Joshua Lee McCarey is missing in action, and presumed dead.*

Ben contacted the military for more information. Apparently, after a long, bitter skirmish, Josh's remaining rag-tag outfit searched in vain for him, but there was no trace. Kathleen was nearly inconsolable.

The news devastated the entire family, especially Jason. Jessie stopped by the ranch often, to sit and talk with her Mother as much as possible. It frustrated her that, when something was really important, she felt utterly helpless.

-∞-

In October, an Armistice was declared in Europe and Americans everywhere were jubilant that the war was over for their loved ones.

Though Jessie was thrilled for other families, *it hadn't come soon enough for Josh!*

It was bittersweet, but heart-warming to see some of the other boys return home to their families. Local news abounded about the commendations some Oklahomans received as a result of their brave efforts in the war. One of the exciting news releases enlightened the world about some alert young Choctaw men who set up a communication system in their native language which the Germans had found impossible to decode. Jessie admired them for their ingenuity and was glad they received much-deserved recognition for their courage.

The wonderful news always contrasted with other, less-happy facts.

The trench warfare, with its mud and dampness, had wrecked havoc on countless valiant soldiers' health. Sadly, many of those who survived the war died of exposure or influenza, as a worldwide epidemic struck.

-∞-

As Jessie dismally drove to the drilling sites one evening thinking of how much she missed Josh, she was somewhat cheered by the brilliant fall foliage over the ridge of hills in the Osage.

She entered a forest of blackjack oaks, the line of rugged hills broken by deep gullies, leading where the hills swept down into a lovely valley. *Where have all the buffalo gone?* She knew how disappointed Josh would be at their decline – he loved the wildness of the country and the native animals that roamed here.

This place was still so untouched, so beautiful, though much of the frontier ambiance was disappearing. She tried to imagine how Spring County must have appeared to the early settlers or even earlier, when only the migrant Indians hunted here. She mused to herself how life in Oklahoma was rapidly changing, and though normally enthusiastic about progress, she wished some of the simpler things could stay the same.

Jessie stopped her car and looked out over the expanse of grassy prairie. The stunning sky mesmerized: clouds swirling gorgeous streaks of fiery red through the blue expanse, as the sun began to set across the wide horizon.

She surmised how Josh could have painted a poetic picture of the colors, the shape of the clouds and how forcefully the wild wind whisked them through the sky. Herself more analytical, not whimsical; she envied people who possessed artistic inclinations. Josh was so imaginative; he found beauty and purpose in everything. Jessie's thoughts grew increasingly despondent, thinking of her brother's young life cut so short.

She sobbed, as she remembered Josh's sensitive soul. *How he might have inspired others. War was such a waste!*

After a time, her angst momentarily drained out; she composed herself and returned home.

| CHAPTER TWELVE |

Jake paced, waiting for the operator to fuel his plane. He was completely frustrated about not getting that Tillman contract. Things were really tight lately and he needed that contract. What would he tell Jessie? She had been so successful, he was more than a little intimidated by the amount of money she made.

He was tempted to stay over tonight and get rip-roaring drunk, rather than fly home with disappointing news. Then he remembered he'd promised his wife he'd be in early tonight -- he'd already been gone for days. He sighed, loaded up his supplies and turned his plane toward home.

-∞-

At the McCarey office in Big Spring, Jessie kept musing about the expression on Jake's face when he left for Dallas yesterday. He was so intent on getting that new contract. It had been rough keeping his transport business going. She knew Jake was so proud - it would kill him if he had to give up the routes and start working for someone else. She didn't really care whether he made money or not - just as long as he was happy. But being Jake, he *needed* his business. She could certainly relate to that.

Losing this one contract wouldn't break him - she was confident in his ability to sell his service to other clients. Regardless, she determined to cheer him up and encourage him. He'd be home tonight - maybe she could do something special to fire him up.

Jessie stuck her head in Roger's office, saying she was taking off a little early today.

When she arrived home, she found Maggie scrubbing the kitchen. Jake had insisted they hire a housekeeper, soon after they moved into the house they'd built. Jessie's first thought was of Maggie, whose husband often struggled to find work. Jessie hired Maggie to come each afternoon, cleaning and starting dinner for her. Maggie was a tremendous help - so both she and Jessie benefited from the arrangement.

"You can go on home for the day, Maggie. Jake will be home this evening and I want to make dinner for him myself."

"I can help you with it a'fore I go, Miz Jessie."

"No, that's all right - surely you have something you need to do this afternoon?" When Maggie hesitated, Jessie teased, "Can't I just give you a *little* time off once in a while?"

"Yes, I got things to do if you's sure; I wanta look at that reader with my boy that you give me. Thankee, Miz Jessie. And for lettin' me bring Jasper here when he ain't in school."

"You know we love Jasper! He's always welcome. Now, I'll see you tomorrow, Maggie."

As Maggie left, Jessie looked in the ice-box to see what she could prepare for dinner. After she peeled fresh carrots and potatoes, she surrounded a roast with them in a large pan and placed it in the oven.

Later Jessie pulled out baking ingredients and stirred them together for a chocolate cake - Jake's favorite dessert. She buttered and floured the cake pan and poured the mixture in it. *Wow; I can still do this.* It had been so long since she'd really cooked, she was a bit afraid she'd forgotten recipes. She tossed a salad, put it in the ice-box and then placed the cake in the oven, also. In the bread box, she discovered a fresh loaf baked that morning. *Thanks, Maggie, you're a sweetheart.*

She thought the cake would take about an hour to bake. That would give her time to take her bath. She put two large kettles of water on the stove to heat, then carried several buckets to the beautiful porcelain tub Jake brought her from New Orleans. She poured enough of the boiled water in to warm the bath. She had a part of a bucket left, which she sat next to the tub.

Jessie dribbled some fragrance into the water, slipped out of her clothes and into the bath. *Ooh, the water feels great*! She loved her bath and especially luxuriated in a soak after a long day. She shampooed her hair, rinsing it with the remaining water in the bucket. Boy, she was glad Jake built the kitchen around the well pump. It was wonderful to be able to get water without having to go outside like a lot of people did.

Though not as nice as some folks' homes she knew, she really treasured this house. It wasn't fancy; but Jake ensured it was well-built; filled with heavy, masculine-looking furniture. Rustic, yet with the immediately-comfortable, welcoming atmosphere she wanted their visitors and guests to experience.

Knowing she mustn't dawdle too long, Jessie dried off and slipped into baggy, comfortable pants and one of Jake's shirts. She checked the oven for her cake - nearly done - then emptied the bathtub. By the time she was finished, the cake had risen; ready to come out of the oven. She ambled back to the dining room, poured herself a tiny glass of sherry, and looked over some notes she'd brought home from her office.

A little later, she thought it would be about time for Jake to be getting home; she checked the roast - it was adequately cooked, so she turned off the oven and left it inside to stay warm. She hoped Jake wouldn't be long. She leaned over the stove, fluffing the moisture out of her hair.

She refilled the tub, then started the water kettle on the stove to heat Jake's bath when he got home. Usually very tired after a long flight, Jessie thought Jake might need some special attention if he didn't get that Tillman contract. He worked hard, yet was so hard on himself.

Jessie entered her dressing room and brushed out her hair till it was soft and shiny. Thinking of Jake again - she should spoil him a little tonight - *what could she do to cheer him up?* Prowling through her bureau, she spied a very sheer gown and robe that matched - a present from Jake. It was lacy and bright red, probably most folks would consider it a little bold for a married woman, but because Jake bought it for her on a trip to San Francisco, she loved wearing it.

She dusted a peach-colored powder on her face and a light touch of red lipstick. No other makeup - Jake didn't like her to look overdone and besides, the apparel she was wearing was racy enough. The last touch: a dab of Jake's favorite perfume to the throbbing pulse at her neck.

True to his word, Jessie shortly heard a plane overhead. She carried the hot water she'd heated to pour in his bath and made him a cold drink. When he entered the kitchen, he appeared pleasantly surprised at her attire. He stood motionless, staring at her.

"Maggie's *gone* for the evening," she whispered as she ran her hands through the hair on the back of his neck.

Jake fumbled for what he'd intended to say. After a few moments: "Jess, uh … I didn't get that …"

"Sh...h," she murmured, then tiptoed and gave him a long, lingering kiss. "You'll get the next one. Guess what? I wanted to cook your dinner myself, just to see if I could still do it. Are you hungry?"

"You know it," he said, as he buried his face in the soft hair at her shoulder.

She put her arm around his waist and led him to the bathroom. "I think *first* I should give you a bath."

"Oh really?"

"Yes, really."

She dropped her robe and stood in only the sheer gown. Guiding him to sit down, she pulled off his boots, then slowly peeled off his socks, shirt, pants and motioned him into the tub.

"I love that color on you, Jess. It really brings out the cinnamon highlights in your hair."

"Well, thank you, sir," she replied coyly. "A certain gentlemen friend of mine bought it for me ... with I believe..." she whispered facetiously: *"risqué* thoughts in mind ... if you know what I mean." She winked at him.

He laughed, and sighed at the feel of the warmth of the water when he submerged. Jessie had him lean back, then shampooed and rinsed his hair.

While he finished his drink, she soaped his back, slowly and lovingly, his shoulders, feet, every part of him. Then she bent over him and began kissing his face, slowly and deliberately, first his eyes, temples, his jaw line - slowly, then circling around and around his mouth until finally, in desperation, he grabbed her and pressed his mouth to hers. Roughly hauling her up, he pulled her into the tub on top of him.

"Jake!" she giggled, but cared less that she was soaked.

A little later, she remembered the roast. "We better go eat before it's completely cold," she sighed.

They dried off and strolled to the kitchen, clad only in towels. Jessie dished food onto plates on a tray and handed it to him. He followed her obediently to the bedroom. She began to feed him, alternately taking bites herself and suggestively tempting him all the while. After most of the meal was finished, he'd had enough of the teasing and shoved the plates over onto the bureau.

He laid her back onto the bed, and then slowly kissed her. Towels silently dropped to the floor.

"Don't you want cake?" she mocked. His answer was to begin to urgently kiss her neck. Jake Trenton knew how to make her lose her control over reality.

Jessie began a mental note to herself. *Tonight was all right, but they probably needed to be careful over the next few days.*

She meant to ask him if he was tired. "Jake ..." she started, but he was swept up in her warmth. He moaned against her neck, "Oh, sweet Jessie!"

She also was lost - could think of nothing for the moment except that she never wanted him to pull away from her - she wanted to feel like part of him.

-∞-

She didn't have misgivings until the next day, when she felt the intense pain in her side that usually signaled she was ovulating. She had checked her cycle on the calendar she dutifully kept, and felt this a 'safe' time. But the pain was early!!

She tried to put it out of her mind, but three weeks later, she knew. Although only a few days late, she knew. She scolded herself: *Why wasn't I more careful?*

She made an appointment to see Dr. Blanchard, but his exam would only confirm her suspicions. "Well, Mrs. Trenton, you're going to be a mother," the doctor validated.

-∞-

Jessie drove home that evening wondering how she would tell Jake. She didn't think he would be upset; they'd discussed this before and he hadn't seemed adverse to the idea of having children. But Jessie wasn't sure how *she* felt about it. Actually, she felt like … crying. All the way home, she struggled with the words she'd use to tell him.

Maggie was busy polishing the furniture when Jessie reached home. Jessie followed her around, moving things out of the way for Maggie as she was dusting. Jessie often would start helping when she needed to talk, so Maggie looked piercingly at Jessie.

"Is ever'thin okay, Miss Jessie?"

"Yes, Maggie, why do you ask?"

"Well, you jest seem kinda thoughtful, that's all."

"I do need to discuss something with Jake, but it's nothing for you to worry about. And … Maggie, you should know you don't need to call me 'Miss.' We've been friends for a long time …"

Maggie sensed there was more, but she didn't push her. When Jessie wanted to talk, she would.

"What would you like for dinner … Mm … Jessie? I's got blackburry cobbler bakin' in the oven -- you's favorite. I'll fix whatever you would like."

"Oh, I'm not very hungry, Maggie, everything you cook is always delicious, so I'll eat anything. I have to admit that hot pie sounds good."

"Well, it's awhile a'fore dinner, so why don't I jest get you a piece of it right now?"

Jessie smiled - *sweet, dear Maggie*. Her friend spoiled her so.

"Maybe just a bite."

-∞-

Jake was late arriving home that evening from a week-long trip to Dallas. He found Jessie in the kitchen, twiddling a fork in her cold cobbler.

"Hope you saved some of that for me, Darlin'," he teased.

"You're lucky there's any left. I've already had three pieces, though why, I don't know. I'm not a bit hungry."

Jake scrutinized Jessie - it was unusual for her to binge on food. Something must really be bothering her. He observed for quite awhile but she didn't volunteer anything. Finally: "Okay, the jig's up - what's going on?"

"Whatever do you mean?"

"Don't give me that - you've got something on your mind. Are you mad because I'm so late tonight?"

"*No*, of course not, Jake. I know those trips take up a lot of your time. It's nothing, really."

"Nothing, huh?"

"Well..."

"Well, what? You're worrying me, Jess."

"Well, if you must know ..." Jessie took a deep breath .... "you're going to be a father!"

"Wha .. what?" After a moment, Jake's face lit up in a huge smile.

Jessie looked blankly at him, not knowing what to say. She wanted to be happy about this, but thoughts of the business kept entering in. *Would she have to give up her career?*

Jake noticed the look, and, trying to determine how she felt, asked tentatively, "Are you happy about this, Jessie?"

"I ... of course, Jake, I know I should give you a family. I'm just concerned about how I'll be able to work with the baby and all." As he looked down at her face, a tear slowly formed and ran down her cheek. She tried to brush it away quickly, but not before Jake saw it.

Oh God, what have I done? He moaned. She'd <u>told</u> him she didn't know whether she wanted kids ... *they should wait until she was ready. Why wasn't I more careful?*

"Jessie, Honey, please don't cry. We'll work this out somehow - don't worry. You can work or stay home or whatever it takes for you to be happy." He brightened: "We can find a nanny or something! And I'll help, too – even ... change diapers, *anything*! Please don't be sad!"

From the next room, Maggie overheard their conversation. She normally wouldn't eavesdrop, but worried about the way Jessie had acted all evening, she'd made excuses about work to be done, and stayed later than normal. Now this revelation was more than she could stand.

She scurried into the kitchen and announced: "No, you ain't gonna hire no nanny, Mr. Jake. I gonna take care of that baby for ya'll." Then to Jessie: "Don't you worry, Missy, you know I will love that little'un like it wus my own, so you jest stop worry'en. Ever'thing will be jest fine." Her smile stretched across her happy face.

"Well, you're so busy with the housework and all ..."

"No, I ain't. You and Mr. Jake is so neat, it ain't no trouble t'all to take care'o this place. And that sw-e-e-t baby will be a lot o'company for me. 'Specially since Jasper in school now."

"That's wonderful, Maggie," Jake answered. "And Jessie, you can talk to Ben and work out a schedule for the office - maybe you can come in later in the day, or whatever ... you're the *boss*, after all, you can set your own schedule. Ben will handle the rest!"

Jessie smiled. She knew Maggie would love the little one and spoil him or her so -- she was the kindest, gentlest soul. Maybe this would work out after all.

"Will you promise to continue your reading and lessons when the baby's napping?"

"Yes'um."

-∞-

Ben was ecstatic when Jessie relayed her news: "Of course, Sis, we'll manage. You take as much time as you need; when the baby comes, plan to stay home awhile if you want. I'll come by to discuss the important things with you. And to see my new little niece or nephew!! Naturally, I'll have a hard time filling your shoes, but don't worry about it - if I need you, I know where to find you. Just be happy and enjoy this time with Jake."

-∞-

Jessie launched into work at the office. She occasionally drove out to the sites and asked advice of her brothers about the latest developments.

She wanted to complete as many of the current projects as possible, so that when the baby came, she could devote time to the little one.

She began to eat more regularly and took a long walk each evening, down toward the river. Even though it was getting a bit colder, she bundled up and enjoyed the fresh air and wild beauty of Mother Nature's countryside. She read a booklet from Dr. Blanchard's office on expectant mother's care; like everything she had always done - she wanted to do the best at being a mother that she possibly could.

She noticed Jake was coming home earlier lately. *I guess this is really for the best - he's so happy.*

Once the baby started moving inside her, Jessie knew for sure that this was right; the maternal instinct took over and she grew increasingly happy that she was going to have this special child - hers and Jake's. She started thinking about names and wondering whether this little person would be a boy or girl. If it was a boy, she hoped he would look exactly like his handsome father. If it was a girl, she wanted to name her Mary Susan after her beloved grandmothers.

She was amazed at the feeling she began to develop for this tiny life inside her. Jessie became very protective of the little one and careful about everything she did, especially driving. She reduced her trips to the sites and asked Jason or Matt to exercise Blackie with a ride occasionally. But often she'd find herself at the barn, stroking her beloved riding partner with a soothing voice: "After the baby comes, it'll be me and you again, okay, fella?"

| CHAPTER THIRTEEN |

A few weeks later, Jessie worked late at the office. Strange … but she thought she heard the outside door. She glanced up just as Jason fretfully materialized in the doorway.

"Well, this is a nice surprise, kiddo. What brings you to the office?"

Jason looked soberly at Jessie. "Jessie, it's Papa. He's real bad sick. The Doc thinks he's had a stroke. You better come right away."

Jessie jumped from her chair and grabbed her coat. As they hurried down the steps, she asked Jason what had happened. Jason protectively held her arm as she descended the steps from the office. "Careful, now," he said. "I'll explain it on the way. Can we take your car?"

"Sure, it's just across the street."

Jason explained: "It'll be faster than the old truck."

When he opened the passenger door for Jessie, she handed him her car key. As they were in route toward the McCarey home, Jessie asked: "When did it happen?"

"About an hour ago. Fortunately, today I was workin' on those fences on the west end. He was supposed to be up soon to talk to me.

When he didn't show up in a little while, I went back towards the house and found him lyin' on the ground. I think he passed out and fell off his horse. We hurried after Doc but he hasn't been able to do much for Papa."

-∞-

When they arrived at the house, Jason ran around to open the car door for Jessie and took her arm again as they went up the steps to the house. As they entered the house, Doctor Blanchard stopped them.

"Sarah, you should know … your father's paralyzed on his right side. This was a bad stroke and I'm afraid there's not much I can do for him. I hope he's strong enough to weather it, but I just don't know. The way Kathleen describes he's acted lately, I think he's already been having some mild ones. I'm going on home for awhile, but if you need anything, please send for me."

Jessie nodded and patted the doctor's shoulder as she moved past him toward the hallway. Jason and Jessie walked down the hallway to their parents' bedroom. They found their mother sitting beside Gus. Jessie hugged her mother before kneeling beside her sleeping father.

"Papa, it's Jessie. Can you hear me?"

Gus slowly opened his eyes and looked over at her.

"Jessie, my Darlin,' where have you been?"

"Papa, at home, with Jake. But I came by here to see you all just a few days ago, remember?"

"You sure you haven't been gone a long while? I've missed you."

Jessie looked at the anxious faces of her mother and brothers sitting around the room.

"No, Papa, I'd never go far and leave you; you know that," she humored.

"Well, I think I'm goin' away, Darlin'. I'm goin' away."

"Sh..." Jessie whispered, "you just need to rest, that's all, Papa, please rest now."

She took his hand as he drifted back off to sleep. Ben fetched another chair for her and they sat next to the bed all night.

-∞-

As the morning sun filtered through the window, Jessie woke, to find her head lying on the bed next to her father. Her mother and brothers sat upright, still asleep. Jason struggled awake and looked over at her.

"How does he seem, Jess?"

Jessie grasped her father's hand and found it cool to the touch. She jerked upright and touched his face - cool, also. She laid her head on his chest to see if she could detect his breathing or hear a heartbeat, but there was none.

She looked over at Jason as tears formed in her eyes and rolled down her cheeks. Jason struggled emotionally for a few minutes, then said: "We have to wake the others and tell them he's gone."

-∞-

Jessie thought it fortunate the weather was fair the day the family buried Gus McCarey. They were all in so much grief; she knew it would have been unbearable if the weather had been rainy and gloomy.

Jake walked with his arm in hers as they followed their brothers up the hill toward the clearing they had chosen earlier for a family graveyard. Ben escorted their mother, who was a bit more composed after her earlier crying ceased.

The day before, a friend of the family dug the grave next to their Grandmother's. Gus' sons and a couple of ranch hands slowly and solemnly carried the coffin to the spot and gingerly laid it down, then moved it over to the opening and lowered their father's casket into it.

Many neighbors and friends attended the short memorial service to express their condolences and leave flowers. When the minister concluded the service, Jessie turned to see Samm Mann standing at a distance, outside the gathering.

Jessie left Jake to talk with her family and friends, walking over to Samm. He spoke with her briefly about the good life their father had enjoyed. "Little dove, your father is now free, some place above, riding the wind with the Great Spirit."

She looked up into his warm brown eyes. Samm had such a pragmatic, calming effect on her; she felt strangely comforted.

-∞-

Jessie walked like she was in a daze over the next weeks. Maybe she was selfish; she knew the others were hurting, too, and tried to keep up a good front, but she felt she was feeling the loss of Gus more than the others. Jessie had a special bond with her father. To her, he was the only person who loved her unconditionally - just as she was, pocks and all, and her Papa had never tried to change her or make her into someone she wasn't. The thought that she'd never see him again was sometimes overwhelming.

Jake watched Jessie intently. He knew she was suffering but frustrated at his inability to help her. He urged her to take some time off work, but she wasn't receptive to that suggestion - she seemed to work harder and longer at night. Ben told Jake earlier that she was fighting with one of the managers yesterday about the proposal of purchasing another refinery, to ease production limits at the one they'd built west of Tulsa.

Jake really worried when Ben related a particularly heated 'discussion' Jessie started with William Masterson, the Finance Manager. Apparently right afterward, Jessie headed straight to her office and laid her head on her desk. When Ben asked if she was all right, she replied that she had a bit of a headache. But Ben noticed she looked a little unsteady later, when she stood up from her desk. Apparently she'd recognized the worried look on his face and berated him: "I'm okay, Ben, just a little tired."

"Just a little tired?"

"Yes, especially of Mr. Masterson." She grinned. "But I made sure he was 'plum hacked' after our little chat!" They both laughed out loud.

Jake, like Ben, thought to himself that she was awfully good at throwing a conversation off the point at hand – probably a maneuver she picked up from that lawyer she worked for earlier. He decided to stay as close to home as he could for awhile. He assigned his most reliable employee, John Bellows, to his important Dallas route and made more of the shorter runs himself.

The next morning, Jake needed to make a delivery run to Duncan. *Should only be gone a few hours.* He was looking forward to seeing Elias Miller again. The two had become fast friends and Jake enjoyed this route as more than just business. When Jake finished checking his delivery invoice, Elias usually invited him out for a cold drink. Jake's normal reaction would have been to accept, but this time he thanked Elias and explained that he needed to be getting right on home today.

-∞-

As soon as he touched his plane down on the rough runway outside Big Spring, Jake saw Jason waiving frantically to him. Jake cut the engine and barely stopped the small plane before hopping out.

"Thank God, you're home!" Jason yelled.

"What's *wrong*, kiddo?"

"It's Jessie - come quick! She's hurting, bad, and the Doc's there with her!"

They ran to the car Jason had driven and raced back to the house. When they arrived, Kathleen, Maggie, Ben, Tom, Stephen and Matt were all assembled. The concern was easily discernable.

"How is she?" Jake asked.

Kathleen walked over to him, pulled him close and held him a few moments. Then: "She's lost the baby, Jacob, I'm sorry."

"Lost ... oh no, *oh no*, what happened? Is she going to be okay? Oh God, I shouldn't have left her today!"

"Sh..," Kathleen whispered, "There was nothing you could have done. You can't stay with her every minute. The doctor said that, I think, the pla.., pla..centa quickly separated from the inside of her womb, so there was nothing to stop her from delivering."

"But it's too early - she's not due for weeks!"

Kathleen softly answered, "Yes, it is too early. The baby only lived a short while."

"Doc said his little lungs was just too weak!" Matt sobbed outright.

"His? You mean I had a son? *We* had a son?"

Kathleen nodded.

"I want to see Jessie!"

Doctor Blanchard came into the room from the bedroom with a grim look on his face.

"I need to see her!" Jake exclaimed.

"Just for a moment, son; she's very weak from the delivery."

"I'll be quiet, I promise - just let me see her."

The doctor nodded toward the doorway and Jake quickly entered the room. He knelt next to the bed, finding Jessie pale and nearly asleep. He quietly picked up her hand, gently kissing it.

Jessie stirred and turned toward him. "Jake ..?"

"Yes, Darling, I'm here."

She cried. "Jake, I'm so sorry; I lost our baby."

"Sh..., you just rest, now, you've got to take care of yourself."

"I let you down, Jake, I'm *so* sorry." She began to sob uncontrollably.

Jake leaned over and took her in his arms. "Please, Jessie, don't cry - it's not your fault..."

"He was so little! I felt him move just this morning. I'm so sorry, so sorry. Jake ...!" she moaned; then lost consciousness.

"Doc! Doc! Please come in here!" Jake yelled.

The doctor rushed back in and taking her pulse, looked anxious.

"Jake, I need to examine her. Tell Kathleen I need her to help me."

Jake nodded numbly and ran back into the living room. He told Kathleen what the doctor said and Kathleen hurried back to her daughter.

Jake sat down and put his head down into his hands. Soon, he began to cry, and, exasperated, staggered out to the porch. The others sat, mute, as if they were paralyzed.

A few minutes later, the doctor came out of the bedroom, carrying a rubber tube and a needle. "Boys, Jessie's started hemorrhaging – badly! I slowed the flow somewhat, but need to try a blood transfusion. I recall that it seems to work best if the blood comes from a family member."

Immediately five pairs of hands began to roll up their sleeves and hold out their arms.

-∞-

When the doctor felt Jessie was stabilized, he told a relieved family he believed she would make it. "She'll probably be very weak for a few days, so will sleep a lot. Keep a close watch on her and call me if *anything* changes."

Jake, grateful Jessie was doing better, walked the weary doctor to his car and asked, "What can I do for her?"

"Just stay with her for a few days and see if you can get her to eat something when she wakes up. And be patient with her, Jake."

"Yes, Sir, I will."

Kathleen came outside onto the porch. The doctor looked sadly at her, then at Jake and said, "You'll need to arrange for … the burial …"

Kathleen nodded and the doctor patted Jake's shoulder before leaving. Kathleen took Jake's arm. "Sweetheart, would you like to see the baby?"

"The baby…oh, yes, please."

They walked back inside and Kathleen disappeared into the extra bedroom. She and MaryBeth returned with a small bundle. His sister-in-law gently handed Jake the tiny form and watched, tearfully, as Jake slowly pulled back the blanket she had wrapped his son in. He gazed down at the tranquil form and gently touched the fine, dark hair and still-warm pink cheeks. The baby looked like he was asleep. Jake unwrapped him a bit more and clutched one of the tiny, tiny, hands in his own large ones.

"How could he still be warm?"

"After everyone had held him, I laid him in a basinet next to the fireplace, Jake," MaryBeth explained.

"That's just the way Sarah looked when she rocked him, Jacob," Kathleen added.

"What color are his eyes?"

"They're dark, like yours. He's got your coloring. Sarah snuggled him and said he was a 'little Jake'. He cried, just a weak little cry, and then he was gone. The doctor did everything he could to try to revive him, but the baby was just too weak."

"I should have been here for her. I should have *been* here!" he berated himself.

"Jake, there was nothing you, or anyone else could have done to prevent this. The doc said he doesn't know what causes this kind of thing -- medicine just isn't advanced enough."

Jake continued to hold the precious package, gently moving back and forth. The others silently sat and watched for hours as he held the little form and rocked.

Kathleen stayed by Jessie's bed, watchful as Jessie slept through the night, from exhaustion and the sedative the doctor gave her. When daylight filtered through the curtains, Kathleen came to Jake and gently took the baby from him.

"I've been making some things for him, Jake - I'll dress him in one of the little gowns. Tom, run down and ask Mr. Peterson if he can put together a small coffin this morning. We should have the burial right away. And Ben, ask the Pastor if he could please come over."

Jake looked at Kathleen with astonishment. *This is where Jessie gets her strength.*

-∞-

Doctor Blanchard thought the procession up the hill toward the small cemetery was the saddest he'd ever seen. Ben and Tom carried the miniature coffin as Jake followed with the others.

Their pastor spoke briefly about their little angel's flight into heaven and that he was now in the loving arms of Jesus.

After they gently interred the tiny container in the opening close to his grandfather, Kathleen covered the little grave with flowers. She cried silently: *How Gus would have cherished this child. Watch over him, my Darling.*

Maggie stayed with Jessie while the others attended the funeral. Afterward, either she, Jake or Kathleen sat round the clock with Jessie.

Later, as Jake sat next to their bed where Jessie lay, he was somewhat grateful that Jessie had slipped in and out of consciousness during the funeral. It would have been too much of an ordeal for her in her condition - she'd been through so much.

Once, when she partially regained consciousness, Jessie screamed out for her baby. Kathleen, sitting next to her, wrapped her arms around her daughter, stroking her hair and soothing her like she had when Jessie was a little girl.

"*Mama!*"

"I know, Dear. I'm here."

Jessie drifted back off again and again for the next two days. When she finally woke up, Maggie was nearby. "Jessie, can I get ya somethin to drink or eat?"

"Maybe just a drink of water; I'm awfully thirsty."

"How bout I fix you's some breakfast?"

"No, thank you, I'm not hungry."

That was all Jessie would say for days. No one could persuade her to eat. She slept fitfully and often would dream and wake up crying. Jake was about at his wits end -- afraid she was really ill and didn't know *what* to do.

Finally in desperation, Jake drove to Ben and MaryBeth's house, to talk with his sister-in-law about Jessie. "I feel this is all my fault, MaryBeth. She *told* me she didn't know whether she wanted children."

"Jake, don't blame yourself for this. You need to be strong now, for Jessie. And I think you need to know that Jessie's reason for not wanting children didn't have anything to do with you. She cherished the idea of giving you this child. And you know how she dotes on Bo, she really loves children. I think … she was just afraid she wouldn't be a good enough mother. She never felt she had enough patience; why she didn't want to become a teacher. Perhaps she simply didn't have the confidence in her own ability. That's why I believe she told you she didn't want children. But you've got to put this behind you and think of your future together."

He nodded numbly, and gently kissing her forehead, bade goodnight to MaryBeth and Ben.

-∞-

The next day, Kathleen asked Jason to drive her and MaryBeth to see her daughter. When they reached Jessie's lovely house, Maggie was anxious and relieved to see Mrs. McCarey.

Kathleen entered the bedroom and quietly took her daughter's hand. "Sarah, Sweetheart, now you listen to me. I know this has been hard for you, but you've <u>got</u> to eat, so you can get better. Everyone is worried about you. Jake's about crazy with fear. I called on Marybeth this morning. She's been asking and asking about you. She's here to see you, and we brought Bo with us. May I have them come in?"

When Jessie nodded mutely, Kathleen moved to the door and motioned her fingers in a partial wave into the next room.

Marybeth quietly approached, clutching Bo's hand in hers. She smiled and bent down, gently kissing Jessie's cheek. But not Bo. In his exuberant childness, Bo immediately hopped right up on Jessie's bed.

His mother had explained to the child as best as she could that Aunt Jessie's baby had gone to heaven and she was very sad. Bo laid his sweet little face right next to Jessie's and rubbed his cheek against hers. He clumsily patted her face with his plumb little hand and said very solemnly, "P'ease don't be sad, Anty Wessie. I wuv you."

Jessie felt a tidal-wave of emotion break and she sobbed as she clutched and held him tightly against her.

In a few moments, Jessie noticed that MaryBeth began to wheeze. "I've given you a bad scare, haven't I? You don't need to be worrying about me - you'll make yourself sick."

"Jessie, you're my dearest friend, how could I not worry? But if you don't want me to worry... [she coughed] ... get up out of that bed and get better."

"You need to take care of yourself!" Jessie exclaimed.

"I know this is a bad time to say this, but there probably isn't going to be a good time, so I'll say it now. You know how sick I've been; my asthma keeps getting worse. I want you to promise me, and I mean, *promise* me, that if anything happens to me, you'll take care of Bo."

"You're going to be fine, just fine, don't talk like that! The doc has been asking for treatments from some specialists ..."

MaryBeth uncharacteristically cut her off, "Bo needs you, and you know it. Even if I get better, I can't give him what you can. You know how he dotes on you; he's wanting to learn to ride the horses and all kinds of things that I can't do. Especially with 'Aunt Wessie.' You promise me you'll get better … for him?"

Jessie looked at her friend's sad face. "Yes, I'll get better for Bo. And for you all – if you'll stop worrying about me."

When MaryBeth sighed and her breathing seemed to relax, Jessie added: "Is Jake still here?"

MaryBeth nodded 'yes,' and Jessie requested: "Ask him to come in, will you, please?"

MaryBeth smiled as she carried Bo from Jessie's room.

-∞-

One evening a few days later, Jessie drove out to the ranch to see her Mother. With the windows down, the fresh air felt good as she slowly took in the haunting beauty of the scenery. As she parked her car next to the house, she noticed a strange car in the road. Curious, she sauntered up the stairs of the veranda.

The front door was open. As she reached for the handle of the screen door, dimly ... through the screen, she could make out a tall military officer in uniform, sitting next to her Mother. Tom, Jason, Matt and Ben were there, also. She tentatively stood at the door for a moment, then opened it and walked in. Thinking it must be a messenger with news, finally, that they'd found Josh's body, she braced herself.

Suddenly, the uniformed man turned around and she found herself looking into the smiling face of her thin, pale, but *alive* brother! For a moment, she felt she might faint, but Josh quickly grabbed her, embracing her so long and hard Jessie thought he would crush the breath from her. As she turned to her Mother, happy tears fell from all in the room.

"We've been calling you about our news, but guess you were already on the way here."

-∞-

Later, over a joyful reunion of the entire family, Josh related to everyone how he'd survived the last months. He'd overpowered a German officer in a prison camp, and then was led by some French sympathizers to refuge. On the run for more than a month, he'd hid for days in a shed (little food, no bath, soap, decent clothes). In one farmhouse, he laid, breathlessly, while German soldiers stabbed bayonets through a false ceiling, barely missing him.

Josh told the family that what kept him alive was thinking about them back home and how worried he knew they'd be. He'd *had* to survive.

Josh had another surprise for the McCareys – he was no longer a bachelor! Later, he finally struggled his way back to Michelle and they were joyfully married. But Josh was exhausted from his trek and wounds and soon came down with a severe fever that lasted weeks, keeping him bedfast and often delirious. Michelle's family tended to his wounds and sickness until they were able to notify the appropriate American authorities. Lost military paperwork further delayed the reports.

Josh also told them the exciting news that Michelle was *expecting*! Michelle would travel all the way from France to Oklahoma as soon as Josh could get the appropriate papers filed. Jessie and her brothers couldn't wait to meet their new sister-in-law and … little niece or nephew!!

She brushed away her tears, thinking: *After so much tragedy, it seems only fair that the McCarey family has some good news!*

| CHAPTER FOURTEEN |

1928

Jake's awfully late getting home tonight. It isn't like him to be this late without calling. Jessie intermittently calmed herself with the thought that the weather between here and Dallas must be rough and he was waiting for it to clear, or he had run into a meeting with a client he couldn't get out of at the last minute and hadn't had time to call. Her thoughts rambled and rationalized on and on.

By the time the clock struck four a.m., Jessie was truly frightened. Shortly thereafter, she heard a knock at the door. She ran to answer it, expecting Jake's repentant grin. *Perhaps he'd lost his key*; but she found Ben and Tom instead, grim looks on their faces.

Her face went white and they both rushed in, grabbing her before she could fall. She stared off, as if into a void. Finally she asked: "It's Jake, isn't it?"

"Yes, Sis, I'm so sorry," Ben mournfully whispered as he held her, stroking her hair.

"How did you find out?" she asked very quietly, like she was responding from far away.

Her empty expression scaring him, Tom struggled a moment. "Sheriff Travis got the news of the crash and came out to the ranch, rather than come directly here. He thought it would be better for us to tell you. He'll talk to you in the morning about the details."

They both expected hysterical crying to begin, but instead, Jessie did a strange thing: she walked to a cabinet and took out a bottle of bourbon whiskey. She poured a large amount into a glass and drank it straight down. She motioned to them, offering them some, but they both shook their heads: '*no*'.

She sat silently on the arm of her sofa. A quiet tear ran down her cheek. "Why does everyone I love leave me? First Papa, then my little angel and now…" she choked up. "Will you stay with me for awhile?"

When her two oldest brothers both nodded affirmatively, she stared glassily at them for a long while, not speaking. Later, she slowly rose, poured another glass of the whiskey, went to her bedroom and quietly pulled the door nearly closed behind her.

Alarmed, they waited until they heard her muffled sobbing. Both stayed the rest of the night on pallets in the hall just outside her bedroom.

-∞-

Jessie walked in a daze for the next few days. Because the plane had caught fire and Jake's state wasn't conducive to a normal service, Ben contracted a quick cremation and burial. He felt badly that Jake's family wouldn't have time to arrive, but it couldn't be helped.

Surrounded by the devotion of her large family, Jessie somehow got through the quiet, private memorial service. Then she remained alone at home, drunk, for days.

-∞-

Naturally, the entire family, especially Kathleen, was extremely worried about the condition Jessie continued in. Ben called Tom each day, saying Jessie had yet to come back to the office. "I really expected her to use work as a solace."

"I know she's had a terrible time these past months, but this has got to stop," Tom affirmed.

-∞-

Tom stopped by Jessie's house early the next morning, prepared to give her a long lecture.

He strode up the walk and as he was about to knock at the door, it unexpectedly swung open and Jessie nearly ran into him. Tom seemed stunned to see Jessie dressed in one of her sharpest suits, her briefcase in hand, as if ready to leave.

"Where are you going, Jess?"

"To work, where else?"

Tom breathed a sigh of relief.

| CHAPTER FIFTEEN |

After Jake's accident, Jessie flung herself like a tornado into her work at McCarey Oil. It didn't assuage the pain she felt over the loss of her husband, but it helped her get through the days.

Jessie never removed the collection of photographs of Jake that adorned her credenza. When contemplating some difficult decision, often she gazed longingly at them for inspiration. She especially treasured one of the two of them giggling, exaggeratedly posing in front of his plane, Jessie sporting Jake's flyer's cap pushed up in a cocky position.

It wasn't long before people urged Jessie to "get on with her life and start seeing other men." She always answered them with the same reply: "I *am* getting on with my life - the business is my life now. And the people at work are like family." She told those close to her: "I'll never feel about another man the way I did about Jake."

After several months, Ben asked Jessie once if she might be interested in going out with Roger Clayton. He reminded her: "He thinks a lot of you, Jessie."

"Oh, Ben, I love Roger ..." when Ben's face brightened, she quickly added: "But like a brother. I can't see myself in a different relationship with Rog. Or any man other than Jake."

"Well then, guess that Tillman guy's out, too? You know, he's loaded, not bad lookin', and has quite the eye for you."

"Ben, if you're lucky, you find real love once. You should understand that. I was lucky."

That momentarily stopped the inquisition.

-∞-

Maggie watched over her friend like an anxious mother hen. And Jessie was pleased that Maggie, as promised, worked hard and learned to read and write. Maggie's diction much improved, as well as her self-confidence, so now she and Jessie concentrated on figures and sums. Jessie sometimes wondered if *she* were more interested in Maggie's education than *Maggie*. But whatever the reason (or her excuse), Jessie simply loved spending time with such a dear friend.

Jessie came to learn the pleasures of small joys: the sunlight shining through the window panes on cold mornings; the smell of pumpkin or cranberry breads she and Maggie occasionally baked together on weekends, Jasper off playing baseball; quiet, companionable talk with people in town. Flowers abounding in the spring. And in the summertime, she relished the refreshing coolness and isolation of a lone swim in the pond behind her house.

The seasons that first year seemed to come and go, without so much notice by Jessie of their changing. To her, one day simply blended into the next, except for those exceptional moments when she took the time to focus on her small joys.

The country was entering a rough time – businesses floundering, people talking about a depression, so Jessie concentrated primarily on keeping the company afloat. She also began to help with volunteer projects, like a soup kitchen, and donated money to a local shelter.

But no matter how much she denied it or how busy she stayed, the weeks and months were agonizing for Jessie. Thoughts of Jake would spontaneously fill her thoughts, occasionally at inopportune moments like the board meeting last week. Tears had unexpectedly filled her eyes, but she quickly forced them back before anyone noticed.

Jessie missed the sound of Jake's laugh, his smell, a comforting arm around her at night, the softness of his hair, his walk. A few times, at a distance, she'd spy someone with his build and gait, and the momentary abruptness of it would wrench her heart like a vise.

Jessie often wrote Mr. Trenton in Philadelphia, purging all her thoughts in letters to him. It was such a comfort when he'd write back, in his aging, shaky handwriting. Andrew remained her connection to Jake. And so very dear. Thankful Jake's brother William and family remained close to Mr. Trenton, she regretted she'd never really gotten to know them. Her priorities always seemed here, in her beloved Oklahoma.

Jessie clung even closer to her family, particularly Mama, and she visited Kathleen often. Although she frequently pressured her Mother to move in with her, Mrs. McCarey continually refused, saying she was at home on the ranch.

A few years before, Tom had married Becky Swinn, a girl from Pawhuska, and quickly started his own brood of boys. Tom and his sweet Becky enjoyed many happy hours refurbishing the old McCarey house. They seemed content sharing the ranch with their mother and re-filling it with a rambunctious pack of sons, so Jessie finally quit bothering Kathleen about living with her.

Jessie occasionally offered Tom and Becky a 'weekend date' by themselves on a Friday and Saturday night, when she'd load up her passel of nephews for an adventure with Aunt Jessie. Her Mother would take the opportunity to visit Jason in Tulsa, where she'd clean and cook, spoiling her bachelor son a bit. Or they'd dress up for dinner at a nice restaurant in bustling downtown and Jason would ensure Kathleen enjoyed a night on the town like a celebrity.

Jessie jokingly demonstrated for her nephews how to 'cheat' at poker like her Papa had taught her. They spent hours of exhilarating riding and exploring the nooks and crannies, caves and hideouts around the countryside.

Sometimes they talked cars and airplanes, or her reading to them about faraway places and adventures like pirates and desert warriors … way into the night. Then, she'd let the sleepy heads doze late, until they voluntarily woke to attempt making flapjacks and hot cocoa together on Saturday. That nearly always resulted in a big mess, as Jessie wasn't much handier in the kitchen than the boys. More than once, Maggie arrived with a "land-o-mighty!" exclamation at the look of '*her*' kitchen.

Sunday begot a different story. Jessie would awaken her nephews in time for church service with the sudden, loud clanging of a metal spoon against a baking pan. After a rousing weekend wrestling with the boys, Aunt Jessie was usually worn out, with a renewed appreciation for parents!

Tom and Matthew continually improved their horse business. Matt lived at a farming ranch of his own a few miles away, where he and Tom could easily collaborate. He remained for the time being the most eligible bachelor in Spring County. Matt was a charmer, with his dark working tan, golden curly hair and chiseled jaw. His gentle love of animals lent him a natural sense of working even wild horses, and neighbors often asked for his help when their fouls or calves were due.

Stephen had become, not surprisingly, a successful attorney in St. Louis. He married Gabriella Nevelle, the gorgeous, bright daughter of a State senator in the 'wedding of the century' and they seemed extremely happy together. They, along with their beautiful baby Sophie, occasionally enjoyed the relaxing scenery via a train trip to visit his family in Oklahoma. There, the entire family would delight over sweet Sophie. Some of Stephen's political cronies were already eying him as an Appellate Judge.

In 1923, Ornery Jason had established his own successful enterprise in Tulsa: *J. M. Petroleum*. Unlike the family business, Jason preferred to keep it privately-owned. He liked the feel of his own reins, even with the ups and downs of financial insecurity he experienced. And Jason, like Matt, was taking his sweet time with marriage.

Josh and Michelle and their two sons, Eric and Liam (who'd sometimes join Jessie for her wild weekend with Tom's boys), lived just outside Tulsa, close to Jason. The bond between Jason and Josh remained strong; over the years, the twins alternately drifted apart, then somehow always close, back together. Josh had returned to school soon after his military discharge. His war experience and harrowing memories of soldiers' suffering prompted him to become a nurse. Though they had adequate money for medical school, Josh felt men patients especially appreciated a male care-giver. He'd been so impressed with nurses during the war; he'd vowed to join that worthwhile profession if he made it home.

-∞-

Jessie never ceased to reminisce about Jake, and often found herself seemingly talking to him. At times she felt comforted, as if he was near and could hear her. She told him how happy she felt that the family members were achieving successes, each in their own way. When she recounted all the good things she and her family had experienced, she realized how very fortunate her life had been. *Even having you and our precious son for the short time we were together, was nothing less than a most precious blessing. I need to remember that and be thankful for it.*

And she believed she'd see them again.

-∞-

Because the company's work force was growing so quickly, Jessie frequently had it in the back of her mind that the local children could benefit from a new school.

The school in Big Spring grew increasingly crowded with the explosive town growth. Initially, the town spiraled close around the area where the mill and local zinc smelter spewed out smoke, close to the river. But as the emergent metropolis meandered away from that low, flood-prone area, nowadays teachers rode the inter-urban streetcars across town to teach at the original smelter town school.

Though excited about the prospect, Jessie also agonized for a long time. It wasn't that she felt the old school not good enough for employees' children; she simply wondered whether it could be a draw for hiring talented new people to Big Spring, if their children could receive a first rate education close-by. She finally proposed the idea with the city counsel. Learning McCarey Oil would help finance a new school; the counsel enthusiastically approved her proposal, agreeing that another school would definitely alleviate the overcrowded rooms at the original school.

Jessie consulted Charles Magee, an architect from Norman, and excitedly awaited his design. When the initial sketches were drawn up and she met with Charlie, Jessie found that he had *two* sets of plans. The first set: basically the practical building she'd initially proposed: a solid, square two-story brick structure, where utilization of space could be maximized.

But it was the second drawing that 'called' to Jessie -- a rectangle brick design, with windows on the inside classes overlooking an enclosed courtyard in the center. The school would have the same square foot of classroom space, Charlie explained, but this design would give the children a safe place to play.

The proposed building site was downtown, within blocks of the busy streets of the growing business district. Charlie explained to Jessie that a courtyard would give the younger children a play yard protected from exposure to the outside streets. He stressed that it would take up more room on the property, but the land area could reasonably accommodate the size.

While Jessie was perusing the drawing, Charlie also hesitantly proposed a small addition (which of course would require additional funds): fanciful, lattice-look eaves on upright beams across the inner courtyard, to act like a type of gazebo covering. He explained that on rainy days, it would provide a bit of shelter for the children playing in the yard. Charlie suggested placing wooden benches underneath, where the children could sit to draw or eat lunch on nice days.

After giving Jessie his proposal, Charlie waited quietly and a bit nervously, all the while watching her thoughtful expression.

"Well?" he finally asked.

"I can't believe this."

"What … do you mean? Is it out of line? Your original idea will work wonderfully; I just thought …"

He needn't have been nervous – when a whimsical smile spread across Jessie's face, Charlie outwardly sighed in relief.

"Charlie, I'll run this by our family, but I'm sure they'll pay for the addition. I … I love this! It's so creative! I can just picture my niece, Sophie, sitting there. She loves drawing. I so admire people who have artistic inclinations. The play yard and that charming covering -- I could never, ever have thought of such creative, yet practical things!"

"You really like it?"

"I tried once, as a teenager, to sketch a picture of a house. It looked like something a four-year-old would draw."

As they laughed together, Jessie determined that they would definitely keep Mr. Magee in mind for future building projects.

-∞-

A few weeks later, Jessie and Ben discussed the latest completion reports on the new inter-state pipeline construction.

"Looks like we're not on schedule, Jess," Ben reflected, frustrated as he glanced over the report. "When I think about this loan ... and we were just seeing light after that fire and refinery turnaround."

Jessie laughed. "I am so excited about this, Ben; I just sense it will be a life-line for McCarey's distribution system. We'll talk with Glenn Wilson in Engineering about these latest delays. He'll know what we can realistically expect. Don't worry, it'll work out."

They looked up as Jason came rushing into Jessie's office. Seeing the alarmed look on Jason's face, Jessie asked, "Surprised to see you, kiddo. But … what is *wrong*, Jason?"

"I just heard on the radio, Jess! The stock market has just hit an all-time low. People are goin' nuts!"

"Oh, no!" Ben groaned. "This is just what we need, on top of these construction problems! The board will really be on our backs now!"

"Ben, we'll handle the board the way we always do - drum up

stockholder backing," Jessie interjected.

"So many times, I wish we hadn't incorporated ... just stayed a private company."

"Well, I have to agree. But ... we'd never have gotten enough investors for all the capital we've now accumulated in the company and we wouldn't have the international business presence we've achieved. You've got to admit, it's been challenging!"

"Oh yeah; oh yeah, 'challenging' is the right word!"

Jason interjected: "I'll probably be okay -- I'm still private. But ... what *you* gonna do about this stock crash thing?"

When Jessie grew thoughtfully silent, Ben interjected: "We've got to keep people from panicking and selling their shares. How about some radio commercial time and newspaper coverage? Explain about how solvent we've been, compared to a lot of other businesses - tell them about the new pipeline project and overseas drilling ..."

Jessie added: "Our stockholders will hang on."

Jason grinned. "Always the optimist, huh, Jessie? Don't you ever get *down* about this business?"

"*Only every other day*," she replied. "Just don't tell that to our shareholders! Let's get busy; we've got to get notice of our wonderful company out to them. I assume you'll both be here, working beside me all night, right?" She grinned.

-∞-

A three-week solicitation battle followed, complete with a blizzard of proxy cards, newspaper ads and calls made to hundreds of employees. Roger recruited clerical personnel and formed a stockholder call center, where they answered questions from thirteen hundred shareholders.

The family's efforts prevented most of the shareholders from selling their shares, but, as predicted, the economic condition of the country took a nose-dive.

McCarey Oil's net income and revenue fell considerably in comparison to prior years, which forced the McCareys to lay off some employees. Jessie became despondent every time they had to call people in and give them the bad news. She and Ben handled them personally, and gave each employee two months severance pay to help their families. She hoped to rehire any that hadn't found jobs, as soon as possible.

The board decided a wage cut would need to be made across the company. The directors balked initially to Ben's suggestion that they *all* take a pay cut, but finally acceded. Employees seemed to receive the news of their own reductions pretty well, when they were told management would be taking a substantial reduction, also.

Dividends were temporarily frozen, which worried both Ben and Jessie, but nothing else would suffice for the time being. Though operating funds were the tightest since the inception of the company, they were able to complete most of their capital projects, and just *hung on*.

| CHAPTER SIXTEEN |

1931

William Murray, Governor of Oklahoma, ordered the oil fields shut down because of the glut of oil on the market. Kansas and Texas joined in an eighteen-day suspension, which raised prices somewhat.

Jessie and Roger labored closely with their new marketing manager to develop a strategy for purchasing small retail outlets from independents that had gone under. Initially Jessie felt guilty about buying properties from people in such dire financial difficulties, but Roger sensibly convinced her that if McCarey Oil didn't buy them, some other company would. She finally acceded and they built their strategy around outlets close to highways near those cities with a large market share for gasoline.

They sent their top salesmen to make commercial sales for crude, some in Latin American countries, which they shipped across the Gulf to their newer refinery. Ben caught plenty of flack for that expenditure even before things got tight; now it seemed a bit of genius. McCarey's share of the gasoline market increased; profits following suit.

1939

With rumor of war again, the McCareys braced themselves to assist with the country's effort. If the U.S. became involved again, energy companies would be invaluable to the armed forces – particularly those with new aviation fuels, chemicals and synthetic rubbers in development. Jessie prayed their country wouldn't be involved again.

Ben and Jessie discussed increasing production and refining throughput in the event they would need to aid their country's effort. As usual when needing a frank opinion, they pulled their best stand-by, good old Tom, off the ranch for a 'consultation.'

Tom believed that it was a tentative balance: yes, they'd want to produce as much oil as possible, but not over-produce the fields. That could prematurely exhaust the gas pressure (which was needed to coerce the oil out of the underground rock formations). And they must consider their throughput capacity at the refineries. A conference with their engineers confirmed Tom's diagnosis. Jessie sighed. *This is not an easy business to be in.* Regardless, she tried to stay optimistic.

While anxiously awaiting news that the struggle might come to an end, she imbedded herself with the research and development department. Tom had suggested they throw research dollars into cracking an aviation fuel with higher octane for sustained flights. If our country did become involved overseas, it would be invaluable to the fliers.

Unlike some other departments, McCarey's chemists and researchers worked well together and seemed to enjoy Jessie's interest.

Jessie was impressed with their 'go-to' attitude. And the Patent Division's thorough research and filing of important exclusive rights on newly-developed products and techniques, which kept them in the game with their competitors.

1943

Profits zoomed for several years, but it saddened Jessie that something as horrible as the war contributed to their success. She prayed that all the valiant American and Allied men and women overseas would return to their families.

During the war, more than twenty-five hundred of McCarey Oil's employees served in the armed forces or with assisting operations like the Red Cross. Forty-two were killed or reported missing in action, with many other casualties. Employees collected gift parcels to send overseas, as well as conducted scrap collection drives, blood drives -- anything they could think of to support the troops.

Appointed to the Petroleum Industry Council for National Defense, Ben traveled to the capital for meetings, along with several of McCarey Oil's research experts. Ben committed most of the company's research and development group to the war effort. The family agreed that until the end of the war, all other interests would be secondary.

Jessie recognized that her presence on the board was generally unappreciated, which she thought unfortunate *(for them)*. In the past she sat quietly and let Ben handle the meetings. But for now, whenever she wanted to speak up, she did. *Let them stew*; she wasn't about to abandon

Ben. He had his hands full on the Council.

Lately, she was becoming disillusioned with the size of McCarey Oil. It seemed to grow impossibly territorial. Everything more complex and extremely difficult to enlist the comprehensive, cooperative approach between departments that was crucial to McCarey's success; the war effort, sadly, apparently the only concern that could unite the departments.

All the while planning a method to coordinate supplies of butadiene to a synthetic rubber plant operated for the government, Jessie and Ben struggled with the department heads, *again*, about the new accounting procedures they needed to implement. Jessie vainly emphasized that they must work jointly, company-wide, to affect a viable plan. Pulling together the diverse financial data needed from so many departments for monthly closing was a huge undertaking. Reporting to the SEC must be clean and accurate; therefore it must be consistently maintained across departments and staffs.

Oh, in face-to-face meetings, the managers patronizingly agreed to the new method; getting reports that matched the control form, in a timely manner, was another thing altogether.

She grew weary of their excuses and feet-dragging. Monthly closings were like pulling teeth. They could take a lesson or two from the fine people in R&D. Many a time in review at the research center, her sincere compliments were uncharacteristically brushed off: "It's the least we can do, Mrs. Trenton. We're all patriots here." What a difference in attitude!

And all those <u>bankers</u> -- that was beginning to sound like a dirty word to her! How in the world had they wormed their way onto the board? A loan here, then another, soon maneuvering themselves in as members. *Liars and thieves*!

She was completely exasperated with Philip Horton, the new Finance Manager, about that last banker he recommended be appointed! And ... Horton constantly quizzed her and Ben: Why were expenses in the drilling area were so high?

Jessie resolutely believed: *He knows <u>nothing</u> about the oil industry.* Even a novice oil man would understand it isn't enough to have oil present in a formation. Many factors must be considered in determining if recovery would be economically feasible: pressure gradient, gravity, capillary action. And dangerous offshore drilling was a monumental expense! *What a thick-headed moron.*

Jessie wondered if Horton had ever even taken a petroleum course, and doubted he had. After all, he only worried about the bottom line -- which didn't mean a thing without producing a product. She determined that, in the future, only those managers with actual oil producing experience, hands-on or field experience would be promoted to vice-presidents. Ben needed to more-strongly influence future board appointments!

She mused that if she were in control, she'd call in each of the department heads right now for a brainstorming session to determine the best plan of action. Then, if anyone balked or interfered with its swift implementation, the appropriate head would roll. She was often amazed at the audacity of some of the newer (and younger) managers' apparent disagreement with the opinion of senior management. Some days she wanted to suggest they "go build their own empire."

Jessie realized Ben was more flexible and adept than she, especially in negotiations with the junior managers. One of her admitted faults: if someone didn't have the experience she felt was necessary, hadn't *paid their dues*, they simply did not have clout with her.

Perhaps it's for the best that Ben handles the board. I'd probably completely lose my temper. She much preferred the hands-on work. At least it felt like she was *doing* something.

Jessie did find it encouraging that more and more women were joining the company. About a third of McCarey's employees were now female – nearly three times the pre-war number and she recognized the negotiating and problem-solving skills of several were top-notch.

-∞-

In spite of departmental problems, fluctuations in the crude market, tax increases, and increasingly restrictive legislative and environmental mandates, McCarey Oil continued to make the tough and innovative decisions necessary to stay in the game. With alternating offsetting margins of 'upstream' exploration and 'downstream' marketing/ transportation to float the other's downturns, they continued to prosper. Jessie was happily amazed: *We seem to make money in spite of ourselves.*

| CHAPTER SEVENTEEN |
1960

Jessie groggily raised her head from the pillow. *Yes, that is the phone ringing.* She wearily rolled out of bed to answer it, and, hearing MaryBeth's worried tone, snapped to attention.

"Jessie, Ben's real bad. The doctors don't think he'll make it through the night. Please come."

Telling MaryBeth she'd be right over, Jessie reached into the closet, grabbed slacks and a shirt and dressed as quickly as possible. She combed her fingers through her hair as she exited the kitchen, snatching her purse off the counter. She *ran* down the path to her car.

Jessie raced to the hospital, oblivious of her speed. Nothing mattered now except that she reach Ben in time.

When she entered his room, Ben's eyes were closed and MaryBeth was sitting next to him. Jessie tiptoed to the bed and taking one of his long, but now-thin hands in hers, whispered: "How you doing, big guy?"

Ben stirred; his eyes flickered for a moment before opening. When he saw Jessie standing close, he smiled. "Hi, kiddo," he replied, before dozing back off for a few minutes.

Jessie couldn't believe how such a hulk of a man could have shriveled up like Ben had done in the past months. *He's just so weak …*

"Bo was here yesterday," Marybeth whispered.

"That's wonderful. But I suppose he had to get right back to his hectic office?"

"Yes, he had an extremely important client meeting, and we didn't know how long all this was going to last, so Ben ordered him back to D.C. He took the red eye flight late last night."

"Sounds like Ben. Always thinking of others."

"Yes, Jessie. It was the sweetest reunion. Ben seemed so thirsty, but had trouble swallowing. Wish you had seen Bo feeding his father ice chips. I'm so glad they had that time together. He'll call today to check in and hopes to fly back again tomorrow."

When Ben woke again, Jessie sat next to MaryBeth, very still, her eyes full of tears. He reached over and patted Jessie's hand; watched as tears silently slid from her big green eyes, falling to her cheeks.

"It's time, kid; you've got to let me go."

MaryBeth began to sob quietly.

"I know," Jessie replied, "but it's hard, Ben."

"I'm going to a better place … you know…" Ben tiredly faltered. "We've had some great adventures, haven't we, kid?"

"Sure have - you and I have been the best team."

Ben motioned for MaryBeth to come closer. He clutched her hand and kissed it. "I'll always be with you, Darling, remember that?"

MaryBeth nodded.

"It's awful nice, having my two best girls here with me." He closed his eyes and dozed, fitfully, for some time. When he seemed to rest, the girls relaxed a bit.

About six a.m., the monitor began to buzz. MaryBeth buried her face against Ben's chest as a nurse rushed into the room to check her husband's vital signs. The nurse shook her head sadly and discretely left the room.

Jessie cradled her arms around MaryBeth and together they rocked until they had cried themselves out.

-∞-

Bradford Buchannan pitched pensively in the massive oak chair at his executive desk, contemplating the phone call he'd just received. It came from Ben McCarey's secretary, relating the grave news that Ben had died earlier that morning.

Buchannan decided to capitalize upon this immediately. He'd call each of the directors on the board personally: *Though the news was sad, the receiver might identify in a positive or sympathetic manner with the bearer.* He began with Kendall Brackman, the assistant chairman, and pointedly mentioned that an emergency board meeting be called. Kendall agreed and they set a time. Buchannan told Kendall he'd handle getting the meeting news to the board members.

-∞-

Jessie swiveled her chair around behind her desk, so she could view the brilliant autumn scenery outside her window. The park was lovely this time of year – a myriad of shades: yellow, gold, rust, and red intermingled with the few remaining green. As the breeze stirred, leaves quietly danced through the striking complementary brilliant blue of the sky.

How Big Spring had grown! It looked much more like a city now, though still smaller than Tulsa. Business buildings stretched for blocks. Coming into the city from a distance, she knew visitors were surprised by the panorama of skyscrapers unexpectedly erupting like wildflowers on the prairie. With its taller height, the McCarey Oil building stood out.

She drifted back, revisiting many of the fine things that had come to Big Spring and how influential this company and her family had been. The McCarey family helped finance the new school and hospital buildings; the community center where renowned artists performed; the large library, with its renaissance-inspired gigantic clock face joyfully booming out musical time for everyone within earshot.

Jessie relished what really made their family's success so sweet: sharing their wealth with others. The past few years, she'd often stayed behind the scenes in benevolent ventures, so she wondered if other people remembered that about her. *I hope the community doesn't think I only care about money. Oh well …* she sighed.

She gazed outside for some time, then back toward her desk, where an assortment of pictures of Jake and her close-knit large family were prominently displayed.

She reminisced back to the beginnings of McCarey Oil Company and tried to visualize the dusty roads, the lean-to buildings. Their family built this company and she was grittily resolute to keep a family member at the head for as long as she could. Now that Ben was gone, she would call on the rest of the family for some support and innovation.

Jessie picked up the phone and visited with Stephen, Jason, and Bo, asking each of them to meet with her at the ranch on Saturday afternoon. Stephen said he would arrange to fly in from a meeting in New York and she promised to pick him up at the airport.

Images of Buchannan trying to suck in the board kept entering her head. He'd convinced them to have him "temporarily" sit as Chairman until a decision could be made on the permanent appointment. Jessie knew what his intentions were: mainly to keep her from the Chairman's desk and *himself* in it.

What a dipstick! What <u>was</u> that ridiculous statement he made? Something about 'continuity of authority' or something about as pompous. He must certainly be insecure if he was afraid of her. Of course, she did have an influence with the other managers. *But why shouldn't she?* She knew this company inside out, had struggled to build it.

<u>I'm</u> the one who took the responsibility (and heat) for that strategic financing during the depression of the railroad spur and the monumental pipeline construction, not to mention all the risky overseas and offshore drilling investments through the years. Why the heck shouldn't I run this company?

Anyone who had been with McCarey Oil any time at all should realize her power behind the throne. Ben knew it and accepted it and appreciated her for her strengths. *What is the matter with some of these other men? Women, too, for that matter (after all she'd done to promote them)? Look at Joyce Hiffler - she of all people should be pushing* for *me to take the helm - after all, she's one of those feminists! And ambitious as heck, but a conniver, not a team player.*

Jessie's first impression of her - that she was a backstabber, held over the past two years Joyce had been with the company. Jessie tried on several occasions to work with her, giving her the benefit of the doubt, but with no success. Joyce constantly tried to upstage the other women on her projects and wasn't well received by any of them. Jessie's only consolation: that she wasn't the one who'd hired her.

Ben was right. We should have stayed private. This company was just growing too big. There were so many personnel and other decisions to be made that years ago they lost the individual contact with many of the people in the organization, ultimately delegating the hiring to Human Resources staff.

She sighed, *just a sign of the times.*

Before she left the office, Jessie had forced herself into a sense of calm and a deliberate plan of action formed in her mind. She smiled at Marsha, who worked as Ben's secretary, now hers, when she passed Marsha's desk in the outside office.

"Have a good evening, Mrs. Trenton," Marsha encouraged.

"You have a nice evening, too, Marsha. And thank you, I will," she responded purposefully.

Marsha looked at Jessie intently, trying to read her thoughts. Then she smiled reassuringly. Jessie looked confident and Marsha hoped fervently that she would be able to handle the board meeting next week.

"If anyone can, *she* can," Marsha said quietly to the steno sitting across from her.

-∞-

The next day, Marsha came in to the office about half past six a.m. and found Jessie already at work at her desk.

"Good morning, Mrs. Trenton, I had hoped to get here early and make your coffee for you."

"Thanks, Marsha, that's a nice gesture, but you're not expected to do that. I made some about half an hour ago. And also … since you'll be working exclusively for me now, I'd like for you to call me 'Jessie.' Would you be comfortable with that?"

Marsha registered delighted surprise on her face, and nodded approvingly.

"Maybe you'd like a cup of that coffee before we get started? Whatever are you doing here at this hour, anyway? This isn't a sweat shop."

Marsha beamed at Jessie. She was the nicest boss Marsha could imagine. She already felt that Jessie treated her like an important member of the staff. Marsha certainly admired Jessie's respect of other people in the office and this simply re-established that opinion. *Too bad a few of the other managers can't act this way.*

"I wondered if there's anything in particular I can help you with, especially the board meeting coming up. Thought you might have a lot of work to prepare for that …"

Roger Clayton suddenly stuck his head through the outer door. "Hi, girls, how's it going this morning?" He grinned like a kid scrambling through a candy box.

Roger, now V.P. of Financial Services, was a favorite with the secretaries in the executive suite. Always so cheerful; friendly to the point of being flirtatious, but the secretaries knew Roger was only teasing them and joined in his banter. Roger actually thought of the ladies like they were his kids. Often bringing them flowers or pastries, the steno pool reciprocated by totally spoiling him, immediately waiting on even his most trivial requests.

Marsha giggled and responded: "Just fine, Mr. Clayton, how are you?"

"Fine, myself. Just fine. Jessie, can we get together for a while this morning? I'd really like to talk to you about yesterday's meeting."

"Of course, Roger, whenever you're free."

"How about now?"

"That's fine, grab a cup of coffee and sit down."

Jessie and Roger began to discuss the upcoming board meeting. After they talked awhile, it was evident Roger felt concerned about how extremely difficult this was for her, right after Ben's funeral and all.

Blast them all! He thought: *They should be more respectful to her.*

"Roger, I'm okay - I know what you're thinking."

"What do you mean?"

"Don't give me that. I know you're worried about me, but I'm handling this. It wasn't sudden or anything; I had faced up to this weeks ago -- it was Ben's time. I couldn't see him suffer any more."

"I know, but the buzzards could have waited a few …"

Roger was interrupted by Marsha's buzz at Jessie's desk.

When Jessie pushed the intercom button on her phone, Marsha explained: "I'm sorry to disturb you, Mrs. Trenton … er … Jessie, but you have a phone call I thought you might like to take."

"Who is it?"

"A lady from the New York Sentinel, a Miss Stevens. She said she heard about what's happening at our company from some woman named Loretta Wingett … Wingate, or something, who's the national chairman of the Women's Rights Society. She wants to ask you about an interview."

"Roger, if you don't mind, I think I'll take this call."

"Go right ahead, Jess, you need all the good publicity you can muster. I'll wait outside till you've finished your call."

"No, please stay. I need you in on *everything*."

-∞-

The following Thursday, Marsha appeared at the door of Jessie's office to announce the arrival of Ms. Loretta Wingett along with Ms. Laurie Stevens, the reporter who had telephoned. Jessie asked her to show them in, then stood and extended her hand to each.

"Please sit down, ladies. May I offer you a cup of coffee or tea?"

When they both accepted tea, Jessie moved to the credenza to pour for them from the steaming container Marsha ordered earlier.

Jessie smiled as she sat down. "What would you like to know about me?" she asked.

Loretta Wingett hesitated for a minute as she took in the surroundings: expensive wood paneling, massive heavy desk, book shelves; Italian leather chairs. Stunning view from the ornate window. She was impressed with Jessie's selection of office décor (though it leaned a bit toward masculine) and said as much to Jessie.

"Thank you. Ben's lovely wife chose the furniture and drapes for me, as well as those of my brother's office, also. Ben and I agreed on furnishings; our offices are similar. We enjoy things MaryBeth selects for us – she has such wonderful taste."

Loretta cleared her throat and ejected: "Mrs. Trenton, I've heard quite a lot about the selection of the Chairman of the Board of this company. It appears you've got your hands full, with the comments I've been hearing."

"Really?" Jessie cocked an appraising eyebrow with her factitious response.

"Well, now that your brother is gone, it's obvious that the Board is going to try to railroad you out of the chairman's position. And from all the research we've done on you, I think you're the most capable candidate for the job."

"Thank you for your commendation, but the decision is still up in the air. I am only one of several vice presidents, so McCarey Oil has many candidates quite capable of handling the CEO position. We may have a big shakeup of management restructuring before we're through."

"Well," Loretta continued, "I'm hearing that you're in for a big fight and I think you should 'come out with both barrels blasting,' to coin a phrase; let the McCarey Oil Company board see what you're really made of! Our organization would like to assist you in your fight."

"What do you base your opinions on ...? How much do you know about this organization?" Jessie asked directly.

Jessie noticed Laurie move around nervously in her chair.

"I've done some research, or, rather, Ms. Stevens has researched your company. We then contacted several of the local businesses and asked questions about the early startup of the operations of McCarey. Most people around here have a very favorable opinion of you."

"Yes?" Jessie nodded for her to continue.

"Generally speaking. However, some of the male occupants of this city feel that you are 'way outta your league' to try to take over as Chairman of the Board. I totally disagree and I'd like to help you, with our organization's backing, to force the board to consider you as head."

"Force the board?"

"Right! You can't let them railroad you out of this position. You can do a great deal for our organization, and the women's movement in general, if you defeat the board's rejection of you as Chairman."

"You assume, then, that I won't get their cooperation?" Jessie asked quietly.

"It doesn't appear so, from what I've gleaned. Laurie talked to another reporter, with the Oklahoma City Register. Bradford Buchannan interviewed with their paper last week. An article will be forthcoming shortly. He apparently thinks he has more influence with your board than you do."

Laurie interjected: "Um … I spoke with several others of your former managers, Mrs. Trenton. Tom Brigance, for example. He told me that he held you in the highest esteem and would not have left McCarey Oil if he hadn't been offered a very lucrative vice president's position at the firm he moved to. I believe that you have more influence here than Mr. Buchannan."

"Well, I don't agree," Loretta added. "I think you've got a real struggle on your hands, and if you don't get some help, you may get 'shot outta the saddle,' as they say around here. I've heard Buchanan referred to as a tough old bulldog."

Jessie's glance narrowed as she studied Loretta -- her smug expression made Jessie feel queasy. Jessie surmised that Ms. Wingate's opinion of Oklahomans probably wasn't very high. *Does this woman believe we're all ignorant and uneducated?*

"So, you think I need your organization to come in here and intimidate our board, is that what you're saying?"

Laurie looked intently at Jessie, apparently sensing that this interview wasn't going well.

"Yes, I think we're just what you need right now!" Loretta

committed to her *faux paux*.

"Well, I appreciate your time, ladies, but I believe I'll handle this situation in my own way ..."

"You mean you're not going to take advantage of my offer!!?" Loretta asked incredulously.

"No, I believe that your organization can be helpful, but after specific incidents, gained a bad reputation for turning people off. I realize your goals of equality for women are well-intended; however, I sometimes disapprove of your methods."

"Whatever do you mean?"

"When emotional intensity is high, certain people sometimes engage in non-productive efforts to change another person's or organization's opinion. When this type of emotion is vented contemptuously, it is usually ineffective, and that is how I perceive some of your past experiences. I don't want to be considered just another of *those angry women*."

Loretta hesitated, apparently perturbed.

"So you feel we would not be effective in helping you?"

"Ms. Wingate, it is never easy to move away from ineffective fighting toward a firm assertion of what is and is not acceptable to us, particularly a woman in a man's business realm. However, I feel that by the time of the board meeting, I will have done what I can to persuade the board of my competence. I believe that women must show their abilities by their experience, not by making an issue of the fact that they're women. Regardless, I will have resolved this conflict within myself, and I will deal with whatever decision the board makes."

Loretta made an openly-sour face. "You're making a <u>big</u> mistake!"

Jessie hesitated, contemplating the most diplomatic way to respond. However, her irritation overrode diplomacy.

"I don't think so, *MS*. Wingate. And I'm finished with this interview."

"Well, I can't believe you're ..."

"Good day, Ms. Wingate. Ms. Stevens, under the circumstances, I don't have any statements to make to the press right now."

Loretta jumped from her seat and started toward the door. "You're making a mistake, a big mistake."

When Laurie hesitated, Loretta looked back and said, "Come along, Laurie, I don't believe we're welcome here."

Laurie replied, "Please go ahead without me, Ms. Wingate. I'd like to speak with Mrs. Trenton, alone, if she'll spare me just a moment."

Laurie looked appealingly at Jessie.

"I really don't have anything to say from a woman's movement point of view, Ms. Stevens..."

"I can see that, Mrs. Trenton, but if you'd extend me a few minutes, I'd like to hear a little more about you. I want to write an objective article, exclusively from a reporter's point of view. I believe you'll think my approach will be fair."

Jessie scrutinized Laurie's expression. She finally decided that Ms. Stevens looked sincere.

"All right, I'll talk with you. I don't believe you had an ample opportunity to speak …"

Loretta stared indignantly at Jessie and then marched out of the office.

"Would you like another cup of tea, Ms. Stevens?" Jessie asked.

"Yes, please. And it's *Laurie*. All this 'Ms.' stuff is getting to me." (Laurie laughed). "And thank you, Mrs. Trenton, for giving me a chance at a real interview. I realize that this meeting was originally Ms. Wingate's idea, but I have to tell you, the more I've been around her the past few days, the more I have regretted coming with her. I have a completely different viewpoint of your board's situation and your position than she does and I'd appreciate a chance to get to know your opinions firsthand."

"Please call me Jessie. What would you like to know, Laurie?"

"Everything!" Laurie smiled. "I know I only said a few minutes, earlier, but I'd really like to get to know the real you, how you started this company, and how you've been so successful. I really admire what you've accomplished and I think our readers would enjoy hearing about your life."

"Well, that's very flattering, Laurie, but I'm not sure where to start …"

"At the beginning, please!" Laurie asked enthusiastically. "I hope my article might give you a little extra support during the next few weeks. I promise to let you read every word I write *before* it's published."

"Do you have that kind of editorial clout?"

"Well, I don't, but my supervisor does. If you'll tell me your thoughts, I'll write a draft and discuss it with him. He's usually very good about giving me freedom when I'm really onto something I'm excited about, and I think yours will be a *great* human interest story."

"All right, I'll tell you what I can remember, but I warn you, this may take awhile," Jessie joked.

"I don't have to be back in New York right away, Mrs. Trenton. If you have the time to spare, I'll stay over as long as it takes."

-∞-

As promised, Laurie Stevens provided a copy to Jessie's office as soon as she completed her news article. She added a note, saying that if Jessie wished to change anything, to pencil in her suggestions and call her. She assured Jessie that her boss approved the copy just as written. Jessie asked Roger to stop by her office and she read to him:

Mrs. Jessica Trenton is, without question, the most qualified candidate to head the staff of McCarey Oil Company. She is to be admired for the unheard-of success that she has achieved, in spite of the fact that this industry characteristically shuns women managers. In fact, when McCarey Oil Company was organized in 1914, the industry rejected women employees altogether...

The copy went on for several pages. After she finished reading, Jessie asked: "Roger, can you believe this? It's so flattering, I'm ... embarrassed."

"It's not exaggerated one bit, Jess. It appears Miss Stevens has a good insight into your personality and abilities. I think this article could be very influential with our stockholders, and, ultimately the board. You let her publish it, without a change, you hear me? It's excellent, just as it is."

"I don't know, Rog', don't you think it's a little *much!*!?"

"Not at all. Why can't you accept compliments when they're sincere, Jessie?"

Jessie hesitated for a while, re-reading parts of the article. Finally: "Okay, I'll let it rip."

"Good girl. Write her a note, giving your approval, then hand me that copy."

When Jessie looked questioningly at him, he teasingly added: "I'll call Miss Stevens myself, before you have a chance to change your mind."

-∞-

A few days later, Bradford Buchannan was busy at work in his office at McCarey Oil. His secretary appeared at his open door.

"Sorry to bother you, Mr. Buchannan, but thought you might like to see this."

She handed a copy of the *New York Sentinel* to Buchannan, pointing to an article she'd circled. Walking just outside the door, she waited quietly, eavesdropping with another steno for a few moments. From inside they shortly heard the expected expletive: "Damn, Damn Damn!"

The two ladies giggled.

| CHAPTER EIGHTEEN |

At the McCarey ranch, Jessie and Stephen huddled together in the living room, intently studying documents. Jessie quizzed: "Is there anything I can do, legally?"

"Well, Jess, the actions of the board will be based on their belief of what's in the *company's* best interests ... financially. If the board chooses Buchannan over you for the chairman's position, you might possibly file something like a discrimination suit. It's a new concept and I'll have to research to see if it's appropriate."

"Really? That seems a bit over the top. I don't know ..." Jessie hesitated, listening to sounds emanating from the kitchen area.

"Hey, I believe I hear the rest of our army back from town. Let's get Bo in this; sounds like he's gabbing with Jason in the kitchen."

"Bo??! Great! Didn't know he was back yet – when did he get home?"

"Jason drove up from his Tulsa office and picked Bo up at the airport last night. He came as soon as he could. Let's go see what that crazy pair is up to."

Jessie hurried into the kitchen, followed by Stephen, where she, then Stephen soundly embraced their nephew.

"Bo! So good to see you, kiddo! And what has my orneriest, er, most industrious? … nephew been up to?"

"Keeping busy with the law firm. Just in case you haven't heard, Uncle Steve ... D.C. is a slightly hectic place!" He laughed.

"Well, good you could be here to help us decide what Jessie's best action plan should be. Jess, I'll always support whatever you do. We may not be able to legally force the board to put you in the chair position, but ... we can make their lives miserable."

Jason cut in: "You've got my support, Sis. And hey, if all this crap doesn't go well, I'll appoint you C.O.O. of *my* company, whadda-ya-think of that?"

They all laughed and Jessie enjoined: "Well, that's mighty generous of you, brother, but I'll have to decline. I think I'd like to give the board and Mr. Buchannan, in particular, a bad time."

Bo looked at Jessie: "Aunt Jess, I'll help with the legal research …"

Jessie reached over and grasped Bo's hand. "I have a special request of you, Sweetheart."

-∞-

Two days later, at the McCarey Oil Company conference room, several men were standing around, talking quietly. Bradford Buchannan moved about from member to member, stumping like a politician with an oversized smile, shaking hands.

To one: "Hello, John, I need to discuss those operations details we spoke about." Then turned to another: "Bill I think you understand how instrumental I was in that refinery coop."

"Kendall, I hope I can count on you today...?"

Kendall Brackman, the Senior Vice President of Operations, replied: "I'm hesitantly backing you as Chairman, Bradford. If things were different, I might approve Jessica Trenton for that job. She's extremely knowledgeable about the oil business and is tough: she performs well in negotiations. I just don't think it's the time..."

Norman Whitfield, another vice-president added: "That's right, Bradford. As for myself, I know I need a couple more years' offshore operations experience, or I'd be stomping for CEO. If Jessica does somehow get majority board approval, I'll support her. I value her expertise and can learn a lot working with her."

Buchannan puffed up. "Well, I see she's seduced the two of you with her polished appearance. But that's simply not enough to run this company."

Kendall appeared irritated. "That's pretty mean-spirited. You surely know Jessica Trenton is a capable woman."

"Well, if it weren't for her brother's influence, she wouldn't even be a *member* of the board."

"I think you've got that backward. We weren't here at the start of this company. There is a lot more to Jessica and Ben's working 'arrangement' than meets the eye."

"What *are* you talking about?"

Norman replied: "Well, just a theory of mine, but I believe Jessica was the real initiator of this company. I've never known Ben to make a major decision without a closed-door meeting with his sister."

Buchannan seemed ready to speak again when he heard murmuring. The cause: Jessie strode confidently into the boardroom. Dressed in an attractive, expensive-looking dark suit and flanked on each side by Stephen and Bo, she seemed contented and relaxed. The members politely nodded toward Jessie, then began to find a seat at the conference table. The low talk died down as Jessie motioned to Kendall Brackman for his attention.

Mr. Brackman asked: "Yes, Mrs. Trenton?"

"Gentlemen, before we begin, I'd like to ask that we allow a couple of 'outside' people in the meeting today. I'm sure you probably recognize these members of my family -- the Honorable Stephen McCarey, Chief Justice of the Missouri Board of Appeals, and Robert (Bo) McCarey, a prominent attorney in Washington, D.C. I'll defer to Mr. Brackman's handling of procedure at this time, if there are no objections to my family continuing in this meeting?"

Mr. Brackman smiled and replied: "These gentlemen have both worked for and been an influential part of McCarey Oil. I have no objection; how about any of the rest of you?"

A few murmurs stirred. Glancing around at each other uncomfortably, they talk quietly, but no one said anything formally. Buchannan whispered to the gentleman on his right: "Well, I see she's armed with enough legal counsel."

After a couple of minutes, Philip Davis motioned to Kendall. When Kendall acknowledged him, Mr. Davis said: "I don't think we should have a problem with McCarey family members attending, even though it is out of the norm for our board's procedures. Let's consider Mrs. Trenton's position in this company, and ... respect to the McCarey family at her brother's passing. Wouldn't you all agree?"

All look around at each other. Eventually, each nodded affirmatively.

"Thank you." Jessie smiled warmly and indicated to Bo and Stephen to take the seats next to her.

Mr. Brackman began the meeting: "All right, let's get to the business at hand. As you are aware, we are here today to select a new CEO for McCarey Oil Company. Though it must be affirmed by a majority of stockholders, our recommendations are generally approved. Bradford Buchannan has graciously filled in Ben's stead since his death last month. However, because of our stock position and the influence on our corporation's credibility, we should appoint a permanent Chief Executive Officer right away. I will accept nominations at this time, but would first like to indicate my personal preference for Mr. Buchannan's continuance as Chairman and CEO."

When there were a few surprised murmurs he added: "I intend to retire soon, so I am not in the running. Do I hear other suggestions?"

Norman Whitfield spoke: "I would like to nominate Jessica Trenton."

Several members began to whisper nervously to each other, but no one else spoke. Kendall Brackman then asked: "Are there no other nominations?"

Another pause. When no other suggestions were made:

"Okay; let's take a preliminary vote …"

Jessie stood and nodded to Mr. Brackman. "Mr. Vice Chairman, since I have been nominated, would you please allow me to again, briefly address the group?"

"I believe that would be in order. I defer to Mrs. Trenton, after which, we'll hear equally from Mr. Buchannan."

Jessie advanced to the head of the table.

"First, and foremost I'd like to say it has been a real pleasure working with you. And watching McCarey Oil Company grow to its success has been the most rewarding experience I could ever have imagined. I was but a headstrong teenager when our family started this company in 1914. We had whimsical dreams, but *never* could have predicted the global destiny of this company. We've survived two world wars, and I'm proud of our contributions to the defense of our great country. We survived a terrible depression, one that left many out of work and emotionally bruised. But while other companies had massive layoffs, we took care of our employees."

She paused.

"People have asked me how I could put my life 'on hold' and devote myself to this company. McCarey Oil and its employees have been my extended *family,* my *life*, for all these years. The job hasn't been a chore for me; it's been thrilling! Why, developing processes and equipment like magnetometers, heat-sensitive photography, our special-technique rotary drilling ... I never tire of learning about this business! Frankly, I wouldn't have missed this for anything!"

Bradford Buchannan pretended to read over some notes in front of him. Jessie's eyes began to fill with tears and several members nervously looked around. She steadied herself and continued.

"I hope that because of the diligent way I have labored with Ben for this company, you will lend some credence to what I am about to suggest."

The room became uncomfortably silent and she paused, dramatically, for a long few moments.

"I would like for you to seriously entertain the idea of a McCarey family member remaining at the helm of McCarey Oil. Because this company has historically been associated with Ben McCarey, *keeping* a McCarey as Chairman should retain the stockholder and marketer confidence we've developed over the years. Our stock price dropped several points this week and we must carefully consider the effect our decision today will make on our company's future."

Murmurs began around the room. Buchannan whispered under his breath: *Well, here it comes*! Several members looked uncomfortable.

Jessie picked up a glass of water from the credenza and took a sip before continuing: "I would like to strongly suggest that you consider ... my nephew, Robert, be elected as Chairman of the Board and Chief Executive Officer. The most effective person to replace Ben McCarey is Ben's son!"

Several members murmured as she paused again. Bradford Buchanan appeared completely stunned.

"As Mr. Brackman mentioned, Bo worked for our corporation several years ago and has a good feel for the operations. That, coupled with his political clout and legal experience, should wield a great influence for McCarey Oil. I have convinced him to consider leaving his *extremely* lucrative law office in D.C. and accept our President and CEO position. That is ... <u>if</u> he is offered the job."

As everyone appeared stunned, she returned to her chair. Kendall Brackman moved to the head of the table.

"Bradford, we'll hear from you now, after which, we'll put the nominations to a vote."

~ EPILOGUE ~

Jessie strode out of the McCarey office building and drove outside of town, thrilling to the feel of the wind whipping through her hair; the top down on her convertible. Heading to one of her favorite places, where the sprawl ended and the beauty of the countryside began, she quickly reached her destination: the small cemetery where family was lovingly interred.

No board problems here, no budget deadlines, just … tranquility. She regularly visited when she needed to make an important decision, or just be alone with those dear ones who'd passed on.

As she exited her sporty, fire-engine red MG (one of her rare indulgences) and opened the rusted picket gate, cicadas noisily announced their presence in a scrub oak tree by the road. As their grating verses filled the air, she welcomed their joyful presence.

This was a spiritual place for Jessie. Gingerly she strolled past each of the headstones – lovingly caressing the names with her fingertips – Mama and Papa's joined together, next to Grandmother McCarey.

It didn't seem possible Mama had been gone two years. *That woman was amazing. Worked in her flower beds that day, in for a hot bath and off to bed. Then just drifted off in her sleep (probably to go be with Papa.)* That reflection brought a smile to Jessie's face.

Jessie walked across the freshly flowered-strewn space to Ben and Jake. Between them lay a reserved space and a small headstone carved with a little angel figure and the solitary name: *JAKIE*. She picked a nearby buttercup and propped it against that adored name, sitting right down in the soft grass before the small grave.

She reflected back on her life -- the difficulties, the triumphs, the pain; the love, the joy, all the people who had been most important to her. After some thought Jessie decided, in spite of the losses and regrets, hers had overall been a good life, a full life. She'd loved passionately and been loved.

Always pragmatic enough to realize no one could go back … or change anything: *The only thing for a wise person to do is look forward. It will be great now, having Bo back in the area; perhaps we could resume our old habit of riding together …* Jessie treasured the time they'd shared exploring the countryside.

She ruminated: *What in the world would my life have been without that oil company? Definitely different*; *would it perhaps have been unfulfilling?* She couldn't imagine it. *Maybe it is time to move on.* Still, it thrilled her to think of the new processes that would develop over the next ten, twenty, a hundred years! Perhaps McCarey fuel and processes would be hurtling travelers to other planets!

Jessie suddenly imagined traveling – perhaps she should take a long vacation and enjoy all the places she'd heard and read about (but never had the time to explore): Europe, Australia. Maybe now really is the time to retire. *What the heck* - fly to Italy or perhaps … Greece; lie on a nice beach, and *relax* for a change. *Hey, I deserve a break – after all, I'm sixty-two years old! Maybe I could take Sophie along ...*

As she rose from her comfortable position in the grass, she marveled again how beautiful are the sunsets in this special part of the country. The deepening layers of vivid purples, hot pinks and fiery red-golds against the edge of the horizon seem to stretch out … forever; longer than anywhere else she'd ever seen, even in pictures. That Oklahoma sky just seemed to reach off into eternity.

After a little while, she decided it was time to get back; it would be getting dark soon and the vanishing sun -- that which infused life and warmth and inspiration in her, would fade. As she hesitated, lingered a moment longer with her loved ones, suddenly, she remembered someone else: Roger.

Rog!! Oh no, how will this mess affect you?! Then: *How could I be so stupid?* She remembered how Roger cheerfully greeted Bo and Stephen, and then quietly slipped away after the meeting. *I should have stopped by his office.* His whole life was as wrapped up in the business as hers, and at his age … *what would he do?* The company was quickly becoming inundated with young executives. Without Ben or Jessie, would Roger stay? Perhaps if she asked Bo to persuade him? *No, Roger wouldn't like that.*

She thought back to their time together - from rowdy school days, through the beginning struggles at the formation of the company, and all the hurtles they'd jumped together through the years. Him always there to comfort her … with relationships, problems, really anything and <u>everything</u>. How would she ever have done it without Roger - always there for her -- always … caring?

It abruptly struck her how very much he meant to her. It seemed odd. She had always loved him as a friend. But, suddenly … she couldn't imagine her life without him in it. And she wanted him to continue to be a big part of her life; no one else quite understood her like Roger. And really … no one else would put up with her crazy whims.

She smiled. *Maybe ... that's what lasting love is really all about: quiet, solid, companionship.* She sighed pleasurably as realized she had time; and so glad she still had time.

Her thoughts returned, as they always did, to Jake. She couldn't believe how she still missed him, but this sudden revelation about Roger ... *Darling, what should I do?*

She sensed his presence, as she'd occasionally felt in the past when alone like this, thinking of him. It was almost … almost … as if he were here, beside her. She would swear she heard him say: "*It'll be okay, Jess.*" She felt warm and comforted.

-∞-

Jessie drove straight back to the office, hoping to catch Roger before he left for the evening. She kept thinking about what she could do to cheer him up. *You know, we could start another business together - something totally different and a new challenge!* But maybe later. Suddenly, she had more immediate plans for Roger Clayton.

| Long Horizon |

-∞-

When she walked upstairs to Roger's office, she found him studying papers scattered all about on his desk. Around the room, boxes lay open, some partly filled with his personal belongings. Obviously, he was preparing to leave the company. She smiled down at him: *Sweet, dear Roger*.

"Still hard at work, Rog? Hey, I've got some ideas for a new business venture -- I'd like to run them by you."

"What kind of venture?"

"Well, I'm thinking … maybe … computers."

"Those big things? Jess, why on earth would that interest you?"

"I'm through with the oil business. It's getting dirty."

"You knew that when you started, didn't you?"

"I'm not talking about dirt, dirty. I'm talking about mean, dirty. This is just an unfeeling corporation, not my company any longer. I'll tell you all about my new ideas. Actually, the computer suggestion is only one idea. But for now, Buddy … I think you've worked way too long tonight. Let's call it a day, okay?"

"Oh well, I really didn't have anything to do this evening, anyway." He glanced back down at his paperwork.

"Yes, you do; you're going with me for dinner and … [she paused dramatically to see if he was listening and whispered] … I think … *more*."

"Um, that would be nice," he responded distractedly, without looking up.

"Well, I've got something for you that I think I should have given you long ago." She smiled into a wicked impish grin. And waited.

Finally, he glanced up.

"Yes?"

Jessie leaned over and gently brushed her lips against his.

Roger was initially startled. Then, watching the deliciously-lustful look on her face, understanding gradually spread across his eyes. *"O---H!"*

Jessie swayed provocatively toward the door. "By the way, what would you think about a trip to … say, the Mexican coast with me? We could get rip-roaring crazy, sip those delicious cold lime drinks … what do you call them…? And swim in the gorgeous Caribbean-Blue Ocean. Of course, that would be … later. You'll have to make an honest woman of me first." She winked at him and vanished through the door like a graceful dancer.

For a few moments, Roger sat as still as one of those Greek marble sculptures. Then, he clumsily switched off his desk lamp, nearly knocking it to the floor as he simultaneously grabbed his hat with his other hand.

Oblivious to scattered papers flying everywhere, Roger leapt down the steps after her, suddenly feeling very young.

THE END

ABOUT THE AUTHOR

Sue A. Townley-Monkress, an Oklahoma native, presently lives on the Gulf Coast. Prior to writing, she held positions in refining, legal, marketing and tax compliance during her twenty-six year career with ConocoPhillips Company in beautiful Oklahoma. She hopes her love for that great State is adequately reflected in this manuscript.

Also by S. A. Monkress: "The Adventures of Will Walker," the discovery-filled Marco Polo journey of a young boy with his father and crazy uncle. (Available on Lulu.com, Amazon.com and Target.com).

Her latest projects are children's stories. Travel, teaching and special time spent with her grandson, Triston, inspires her to share her love of reading.